SWITCH HITTER
PART TWO

50/50 Crew: 'Til Death Do Us

Copyright © 2024 by Karriem Bilal Muhammad.

All rights reserved. No part of this publication may be reproduced, distributed, or transmitted in any form or by any means, including photocopying, recording, or other electronic or mechanical methods, without the prior written permission of the publisher, except in the case of brief quotations embodied in critical reviews and certain other noncommercial uses permitted by copyright law. For permission requests, write to the publisher, addressed "Attention: Permissions Coordinator," at the address below.

Move The Chains Publishing

Publisher's Note: This is a work of fiction. Names, characters, places, and incidents are a product of the author's imagination. Locales and public names are sometimes used for atmospheric purposes. Any resemblance to actual people, living or dead, or to businesses, companies, events, institutions, or locales is completely coincidental.

Book Layout ©2024 Urban House
Copyright © 2024
First Edition 2024 – Switch Hitter 2: 50/50 Crew: 'Til Death Do Us
Author: Karriem Bilal Muhammad

PROLOGUE

After years and years of bloodshed, countless wars, victories, and slaughters over their enemies, Gorilla never could imagine doing anything else but making millions with his brothers in the 50/50 Crew and continuing to prosper. Yet here he was, with pressure on him from his soul mate, Jamaica, to leave the life alone and separate himself from the 50/50 Crew altogether in order to avoid possible future indictments or a conspiracy case. Jamaica being in his ear day in and day out about quitting the game reminded him of how close he came to losing her a few years ago when the 50/50 Crew were at war with the Butcher Boys over complete control of Essex County. The Butcher Boy soldiers had kidnapped her and raped her. Then they left her for dead in an abandoned warehouse, but she had managed to cling to life and now she wanted him out of the game. The game that made him, brought him closer to his brothers, made him millions, and success beyond his wildest dreams. The game was in his veins. The hustle, the muscle, intimidating the competition, the profits, growing with his team as responsible businessmen (both illegal and legal); every aspect of the game was a drug to Gorilla.

As he stood in the confines of a cellar located at some secluded hideaway, Gorilla held a brand-new 16-gauge shotgun to the head of a man strapped securely to a chair with a rag stuffed in his mouth, and a potato sack over his head. He gripped the shotgun with extremely strong hands and pumped a cartridge into the chamber of the deadly weapon. The eerie echo could be heard all over the enormous basement of Tito's mansion in Miami. Marko and Tony left Gorilla alone with the man because they had other extremely important business to handle for Tito. The basement doubled as a torture chamber for obtaining information from the opposition and eventually making bodies disappear.

"You killed my brothers you bitch ass nigga!" barked Gorilla at the whimpering figure. "You and your motherfucking people are responsible for causing my lady permanent damage pussy, and now it's time to pay the motherfucking piper bitch!" continued an angry Gorilla.

"Mmm! Mmmm! Mmmmmmmmm!" came the mumbles of the hooded and gagged captive. "Mmm! Mmmm! Mmmmmmmm! Mmm!" came the noises again from the whimpering, terrified person even louder this time.

"What? You fucking bitch!" yelled an infuriated Gorilla, snatching the hood off the prisoner and revealing a terrified Baby Hatchet. "Shut all that motherfucking noise up playboy, you know what it is bitch! It's fucking curtains for you!" Gorilla barked, swinging the back of the shotgun in the direction of the now visibly shaking Baby Hatchet, connecting with his nose and shattering it completely. Baby Hatchet tried to yell out in pain, but his cries were stifled by the gag. Tears ran down his face as he pissed himself.

"I don't want to do this anymore!" he yelled out. "You killed my baby sister Dolly and threatened my family cocksucker. But you will bring harm to no one else motherfucker!" he continued. "I don't want to do this shit anymore!" he yelled even louder this time, more emotional.

Then, without hesitation, he put the massive shotgun to the face of Baby Hatchet and rested the barrel on his smashed nose. Then he pulled the trigger, putting an end to the nemesis that plagued the 50/50 Crew for far too long.

Chapter 1
Gorilla

Far from a gentle giant now, Gorilla was very peaceful and respectable when he was a younger dude; always courteous and friendly to people.

His parents were very strict and prominent individuals, and they both were involved with politics back in their native homelands so they tolerated no nonsense whatsoever. He always commanded respect because he gave it but when you are young and just coming up in the world, the elements of the streets sometime make the monster come to the surface.

When he began to get teased about the fact that he was of mixed race, due to his Nigerian and Jamaican bloodlines, around the time that he was thirteen or fourteen years old, he started to flex his young muscle and impose his presence on the rude and disrespectful. Day in and day out, he was the cause of somebody's nose or jaw being broken, and he was responsible for smacking the shit out of some big mouth jokers at least three times a day.It earned him a reputation and he became feared by many around his neighborhood. Still, he was not a bully.

Some called him "Big Man," others just called him Africa." Very few called him by his given name, and no one ever called him out of his name anymore. He had big, long arms that hung past his pockets when he stood up, and ever since he was fourteen years old one would swore that he grew about an inch and gained at least ten pounds every year until he was twenty-two years old. He was heavy into wrestling, and was very addicted to the weight room in high school as well. Every other day he was in the weight room, even on the weekends. Due to the fact that he was already tall, he began to swell up quickly and at his young age, he was bigger than the average man of twenty-five years old; he was huge.

It was during his freshman year that he met his soul mate, Jamaica.

Her given name was Doris Owen, and she was originally from Kingston, Jamaica. She was two years older than he was and she was the star of their high schools' Women's Varsity Volleyball team, standing at 6' 1" and weighing 210 pounds at just sixteen years of age. She had a very shapely body and beautiful complexion due to her island roots, and she was always the center of attention, getting advances from all of the basketball and football players that were seniors. Still, she only had eyes for Winston Graham. The one that soon would be known to all as Gorilla.

By sheer coincidence, one day after school while young Gorilla was leaving the weight room on his way to the basketball courts that were adjacent to the high school, just seconds later Jamaica was leaving the gymnasium, and was there to warn young Gorilla that he was being quickly approached by four individuals that looked as if they were out to do him some harm.

"Watch out Africa, they behind you!" she screamed out.

Young Winston then turned around quickly, throwing his backpack to the ground and low- rushed the first two that were the closest to him like a middle linebacker, knocking them to the ground once his vise-like grip had their legs.

"What's up bitches?" yelled young Gorilla, his face menacing and his eyes flashing evil. He jumped up quickly and kicked the closest one to him in the face, then turned to the other one and knocked him out with a right jab to the chin. The first two that went down from the tackle were now crawling trying to get away. They were terrified at how the script was flipped and he was handling all four of them. Young Gorilla wasn't hearing any of that though. He was in "destroy-mode" now and there was no stopping him.

"Don't run now pussies! Get the fuck over here!" he yelled as he ran them down and tore into their asses some more. "Yeah bitches! You don't want these fucking problems!" young Gorilla screamed again as he fucked them up some more; one by one, two by two, three at a time. He had turned the attack and was now whooping their asses for ganging up on him. They were between five foot three inches and five foot seven inches tall, and young Gorilla was six-foot two! Then, out of nowhere, three small but loud gunshots rang out. Pop! Pop! Pop! And three of the four punks fell to the ground screaming in agonizing pain, grasping at their body parts that were on fire from the bullets.

Then, out of nowhere, as the punks screamed in pain, a familiar face appeared smiling bloody murder. Young Winston did not know him personally. He had only known of him as young Kelvin that hustled hard and got money in the hood. He was three or four years older than young Winston. Then he spoke.

"The only reason why I'm going to let you walk away from this is so that you can warn other dumb motherfuckers like you not to fuck with my man Gorilla, you hear me pussy?" barked young Speechless, with his right arm extended and twenty-two revolver pointed at the kids' face. The young punk took off running and left his friends behind.

"Hey, thanks man I appre—" young Gorilla started to thank him, but was cut off abruptly.

"Hold up homeboy. I am not done with these pussies yet," said young Speechless. Pop! Pop! Pop! Three gun shots went off again. He turned to each kid and shot them again, leaving young Gorilla and young Jamaica speechless, and the three punks for dead.

As they walked away, young Gorilla asked young Speechless who he was and why he had called him Gorilla back there when the kids tried to jump him. They both then noticed young Jamaica walking behind them, but kind of with them.

"Is this your girlfriend G?" asked young Speechless. Young Gorilla slowed down so that she could catch up with them, then he smiled at her and put his arm around her shoulder then said,

"Yeah man, this is my girl, Jamaica. My name is Winston by the way," responded young Gorilla pulling her closer to him.

"I called you Gorilla because from this point on that's what you are to the motherfuckers that are not on your team, a motherfucking Gorilla! It is who you are and my name is Speechless," he said, extending his right hand towards young Gorilla and shaking his hand firmly.

After that first encounter, they were best homeboys and tight as biological brothers. Young Speechless showed young Gorilla the ropes and intricate details about the drug game but most importantly, he taught him the importance of fear and intimidation.

Young Speechless had driven young Gorilla and his sweetheart to the nearest

McDonald's for big macs, fries, and shakes that day of the shooting at the high school. They sat inside and ate their food, enjoying their shakes (though young Gorilla mentioned that he loves White Castle's shakes also), and they talked about why what went down happened in the first place. He told young Gorilla and young Jamaica that he had been watching the whole ordeal from the time she had screamed out to him to watch his back. He had been in his Mercedes CLK convertible with the seat reclined all the way back, just watching the young G handle himself. He had already decided to recruit the youngster for his new drug crew; HBH which stood for "Half-Breed Hustlers," and would be comprised of all young gangsters that were of mixed race because at one point or another in their lives, someone said or did something negative to them regarding their ethnic origin. Young Speechless had the money, the resources, and the savvy to put together the perfect team. He congratulated young Gorilla that day on handling himself well, and also welcomed him to the family. After they had dropped off his girlfriend at her house, the two of them began to cruise the streets and observe the areas that young Speechless said he wanted to either pioneer or flat-out takeover.

They drove around for about an hour through Irvington, East Orange, North Newark, Down the Hill, Up the Hill, Weequahic, Maplewood, South Orange, West Orange, Caldwell, and Hillside. It was all just a cruise on the freeway away. Either five or ten minutes apart was each town and major city. He explained that more plans and details would surely come in the near future, as well as him meeting his other brothers in the family: Shorty Slice, Pretty Boy, and Chinky.

Everywhere that they went, young Speechless had young Gorilla hopping out of the car and fucking people up that owed him money or were standing on a strip that they weren't supposed to; making the block extra hot when they didn't even hustle out on that strip. Still, he wasn't a bully though, he was a regulator. One that regulated all the bullshit and enforced the rules to the fullest!

He didn't play any motherfucking games either, young Gorilla was good at his job. As a matter of fact, he was a natural. More money was paid on time and less excuses was offered once young Gorilla was on the team, and nobody was ducking them either, because if you were caught on the run by him then that was your ass! He had already damn near killed several individuals as the main enforcer in the young HBH Crew and he was constantly on top of every situation that needed to be regulated. He was the very last of the crew to be recruited. He was the seal.

When he first met his brothers in the HBH Crew, he wasn't apprehensive at all back then because young Speechless had prepared him for whom he would be meeting, and gave him a basic rundown on everyone's origin and purpose in the organization.

"Chinky is the very first member that I found for HBH. He was thorough, real, trustworthy, and a lone wolf. He had all that was required in this family to be successful. He didn't fuck with everybody, but he fucked with anybody if you fucked with him, point blank. He didn't give a damn what you were or what gang you claimed. His gangster was always manifested when it came down to it!" said young Speechless. "When I took a brief fall and had to do some jail time, Chinky held things down for me. three motherfucking years!" Shorty Slice was the next to be put down right after Chinky.

Although Slanted-Eyes never been pinched before, he carries himself as if he has been through Rahway and Trenton on different bids. Shorty Slice on the other hand, is a motherfucking loose cannon and will kill anybody in broad daylight. Fuck who sees him, as long as the enemy's is gone forever . A short fuse and uncontrollable temper. Those two combined are a very dangerous combination," young Speechless continued. "He will cut a motherfucker in the face with a blade even if they were holding their child in their arms if they owed that money or violated in any way. He just don't give a fuck! He always said everyone respects a crazy motherfucker!

I met him when Shorty Slice and I were down doing a juvenile bid which bring us to Pretty Boy; the coolest and most connected member of the family by far. But you will see for yourself just how real home boy is my brother. He also was put down with the family while we all were locked up. Pretty Boy is Dominican and Puerto Rican, Chinky is Korean and Puerto Rican, you are Nigerian and Jamaican, I am Black and Italian and Shorty Slice is mixed with Guyanese and Belize," he said. "This is what makes us the Half-Breed Hustlers. No one really knows the meaning of HBH or what it really stands for but us," young Speechless continued.

"Why can't we just be the 50/50 Crew?" asked an inquisitive young Gorilla.

"Huh? What did you say?" asked young Speechless as they walked through the door to the game room of their club, on the way to meet everyone else.

"I said since we are all 50% this and 50% that, instead of Half-Breeds, why can't we just be the 50/50 Crew?" repeated young Gorilla.

"I like that," came the voice of young Chinky, meeting young Gorilla for the first time shaking his hand and embracing him as a brother.

"Yeah, the 50/50 Crew. I like that too bro," chimed in young Pretty Boy, also shaking young Gorilla's hand and embracing him as a brother.

"Really?" asked young Speechless, their leader. "You gangsters like the 50/50 Crew over HBH? Let it be known now, we are all brothers here!" voiced young Speechless again.

"Yeah, big bro, that's slick and I think it should stick. The 50/50 Crew!" spoke young Shorty Slice, introducing himself to young Gorilla and embracing him as all the brothers before him did. "I like that name for us a lot Speechless, let's run with that bro!" young Shorty Slice said to young Speechless again.

"Alright then everybody. Gather around and swear this oath on this day: That we won't let anything come between us, and I mean anything. That we will play hard from the play yard to the graveyard and that we will protect and honor one another as if we came out the same god damn pussy!

And always remember *this*, my brothers in the 50/50 Crew. We leave no witnesses and when we go to war, as long as everyone is dead, we don't have to worry about any retaliation. We kill all them bitches! Understood?" asked young Speechless, his face displaying a serious look.

"50/50 Crew from the play yard to the graveyard!" they all chimed in unison, raising their handguns to the ceiling.

That was a mere few months ago, and now here he was, regulating the day-to-day affairs of the young 50/50 Crew, imposing havoc on anyone that owed money or stood in the way of the crew making more money. They all looked up to young Gorilla, literally. He was the biggest of all of them at just fifteen years old, now standing at six foot three" and weighing two hundred and forty pounds. Everyone else was shorter than he was, and smaller, even young Speechless who was six-foot-one at the time and weighed two hundred and twenty pounds at eighteen.

Before young Gorilla became family, young Speechless was the biggest in the 50/50 Crew. Young Pretty Boy was just five foot seven and one hundred and seventy five pounds at sixteen, young Chinky was five foot ten" and around one hundred ninety pounds at sixteen because he always worked out, and young Shorty Slice was only five foot five" and weighed just one hundred and fifty seven pounds, but he was deadly as shit at just nineteen years old. For them all to be some young g's, they started making a lot of money and gaining the attention of many older big-time drug dealers that envied them with a passion! Everyone had at least two cars each or a car and a truck of their choice as well as plush apartments in different locations because you never let anyone outside of the family know where you laid your head down at night or where your family was located. Young Gorilla, young Pretty Boy, and young Shorty Slice were all into jewelry really heavy and were always seen as motherfuckers that got money in the hood for that reason. They were always shining and boasting that bling! It was their statement, hell. They were young and fucking balling out of control! Every week they were copping new shines, rings, or earrings. They had more diamonds than the most accomplished rappers or musicians in the country and they were "stars" in their areas. Unfortunately, jealousy and envy are poisons that infect the weak, the insecure, and the competition.

Chapter 2
Leadership

After numerous threats to his young 50/50 Crew members, an actual attempt on Pretty Boy's life (as some Dominican goons from Washington Heights came across the water and tried to take over the entire North Newark), and other gangs coming up trying to get a chunk of Essex County, young Speechless was fed up and decided to send a message. Actually, numerous messages.

First order of business was that the motherfuckers responsible for the attempt on young Pretty Boy's life be dealt with, and they would soon find out that the cost for fucking with a member of the 50/50 Crew was your life!

All five of the young 50/50 Crew members rode over to Manhattan in two vans, loaded with weapons and firebombs. When they reached the designated street in Washington Heights, young Gorilla slid open the van door while young Chinky and young Pretty Boy lit and threw Molotov cocktails unto the sidewalks as young Shorty Slice sprayed everybody on both sides of the street that were running and ducking, with bullets from a Mac eleven submachine gun. When the clip was empty, young Speechless who was driving the van, handed young Shorty Slice another loaded weapon so that he could continue the onslaught.

Once young Pretty Boy, young Chinky, and young Gorilla were done throwing the six firebombs, they started firing shot as well from two Intra tech nine machine guns and another Uzi. While the van cruised at a slow speed of ten miles per hour, the 50/50 Crew did much damage to the block of the enemy as they destroyed property, jeopardized security, and ended lives.

In the end, there were six brownstones damaged and fifteen people dead: two bosses, four lieutenants, two mothers, three children, and four other drug dealers that were just on the block copping their packages from the various spots on the busy strip. As they sped up and fled the block after the assault, only then was there an attempt to shoot back at the pitch-black van with the fake New Jersey license plates but it was too late to retaliate, because they had done damage and disappeared, leaving devastation and chaos in their departure.

Once they were done taking care of business in New York, the young 50/50 Crew dipped off to switch clothes and reload their gear. They torched the van even though it wasn't stolen. Still, they risked nothing. Therefore, they burned it for any fingerprints or shell casings that may have been left behind.

Once they regrouped, had changed entirely, and got their heads right, they got in three different rentals and headed down the hill and across to the Weequahic section of Newark. There was too much talk in the air about how much money the little hustlers were getting and talk of "kidnapping" or "torturing" one of the little motherfuckers to teach them a lesson and run them off of the turf. Young Speechless wasn't having any of that! The orders were given, and the three cars split up.

Young Gorilla rode with young Speechless into the block of Elizabeth Avenue. From the highway all the way to Lyons Avenue was controlled by Terrance Terry and his young mob of "don't give a fucks," and he had indirectly threatened young Speechless and his crew by saying that he was going to deal with anyone trying to get money that wasn't of his family or organization. And by deal with them, he indeed meant kill them.

Young Speechless had heard that shit in his ear one too many times. It was time to end this motherfucker Terry and flood his territory with the work of the 50/50 Crew, fuck getting permission from an older motherfucker or any motherfucker for that matter.

He and young Gorilla parked around the corner from the barbershop that Terrance Terry owned and maneuvered out of, and as soon as they got out of the car, they started shooting Terry's goons left and right. They didn't even know what had hit them because they were so comfortable down in that area for so long.

People came running from the Towers that he had on post, but they were no match for young Gorilla and the AK47 he was letting off in their direction. Body after body dropped as young Gorilla chopped them down and sent most of them fleeing across the street into Weequahic Park for cover amongst the many trees. Young Speechless ran into the barbershop shooting everything, and if you were in there at that particular time, then you were just out of luck because he shot every one of the four customers and three barbers before he trapped Terrance Terry in the back corner.

"Terrance T. you are done, motherfucker. 50/50 Crew rule this shit now bitch!" spoke young Speechless as he emptied the remainder of the 9mm Uzi clip into Terrance Terry, finishing him once and for all.

Meanwhile, young Chinky and young Pretty Boy hit the blocks of Bergen Street and Lyons Ave. and cleared that shit the fuck out when they caught Mike-Mike from Chancellor Avenue Crew in the pizza parlor and splattered him against the walls and counter of the popular eatery. Young Pretty Boy caught a flesh wound to the back of his right shoulder when one of the soldiers holding down Mike-Mike shot at them from the rooftop across the street with a twenty-two caliber rifle.

If it weren't for the first two bullets hitting the windows and young Pretty Boy shifting his position, he would have probably gotten shot through the back of his head. Young Chinky snapped when he saw his comrade shot, so he turned in the direction of the rooftop and squeezed almost thirty rounds from the Calico he was wielding at the shooter on the roof, tearing up the tar, aluminum flashing, and bricks that held that small part of the roof together. As he heard the shooter scream out in pain, a Newark cop car was coming around the corner, and had obviously gotten the call from the pizzeria that shots were being fired and someone had been killed because he could clearly hear more sirens approaching fast!

"Come on P.B. let's get the fuck out of here. You good?" yelled young Chinky checking on his brother, as he started shooting up the doors and windows of the police car bringing them to a halt. They had parked around the corner on Weequahic Avenue in between Bergen and Elizabeth and by the time more cops had pulled up on the scene at Lyons Avenue, young Pretty Boy and young Chinky were already on Elizabeth and Chancellor, hauling ass into Hillside, New Jersey.

Young Shorty Slice was given a solo mission and he was told to take out Mustafa that ran the Maple Avenue/Chancellor Avenue area. Mustafa, or Big Mu as many called him, was not on the block at the time the young 50/50 Crew executed their annihilation plans for takeover in the Weequahic section. He was fucking some fine-ass redbone chick that young Pretty Boy use to fuck on a regular basis. Of course, young Pretty Boy got the info and the lay-out of her place, even got the key to the front door from the bitch, which of course, he had given to young Shorty Slice.

Big Mu was 6'4" and weighed about 300 pounds because he was a failed semi-pro linebacker at thirty years of age and decided to impose his bullying on the young hustlers in the area and make them all work for him. Every day, he had chosen to embarrass one of his workers and make an example out of them in public. It worked psychologically because no one was ever out of line and didn't want to be the one to get embarrassed by Big Mu.

Young Shorty Slice parked directly in front of her house, got out and got his tools out of the trunk of the rental car. Then he walked up the stairs and listened for a few seconds. He could hear the young 19-year-old redbone screaming out in pleasure or pain from Big Mu and he knew now was the time to make his move. He used the key that was given to him by young Pretty Boy and got in the house with no problems.

Taking out his silenced pistol and scalpel out of his small bag, he crept up the stairs and into the bedroom while the older kingpin was eating out shorty's pussy. It was only supposed to be Big Mu that was killed on that day, but the 50/50 Crew never left any witnesses behind alive.

When she saw young Shorty Slice enter her room, she pulled Mustafa's head closer to her treasure, smothering him in her juices as he greedily lapped up her cream. As soon as she started to scream out in ecstasy, young Shorty Slice shot her twice; one through the mouth and one to the forehead. Then he lowered his pistol and shot Big Mu four times before slicing his throat from ear to ear. He left the house the same way he had come in, quietly.

When they met back up at the headquarters, everyone was relieved that all young Pretty Boy had sustained was a flesh-wound to the top of his right shoulder. The bullet literally grazed him. Reports were in, mission was a success. Now all they had to do was wait a week, then flood the Weequahic section with top-notch product and lock down the area.

"Well done brothers. We took care of business out there today for sure!" said their young leader. "Now motherfuckers will witness the real power of the 50/50 Crew. Nobody eats in these areas unless they work for us or buys from us, point blank period," young Speechless continued.

"Yeah, motherfuckers have to KNOW that we are here to stay. No time for games in these streets!" yelled young Shorty Slice.

"Pretty Boy you alright bro?" asked young Gorilla, concerned about his brother.

"Yeah man, I'm cool. Shit just burns like hell for real. After the Doc gets here and patches me up, I should be fine. Somebody light one up and pass that shit to me ASAP please!" expressed an injured young Pretty Boy.

"You two get Double-T out of here or what? That bastard has been getting on my nerves with all of them indirect threats and shit," asked young Chinky of young Speechless and young Gorilla about Terrance Terry.

"Of course, we did. That pussy had to be dealt with for sure slanted eyes. We handled him and at least ten of his people. They will all be in the Star-Ledger this week and the obituary column soon after!" said young Speechless.

"We cleaned house on them pussies bro and now most of the Weequahic section is fucking ours! Let's get this motherfucking money!" spoke young Gorilla, anxious to put in more work.

From that point on, the 50/50 Crew was unstoppable in Essex County. They branched out into so many different territories that it didn't make any sense how fast they blew up in the drug game.

As they grew older, they grew richer and richer. Much more powerful than they ever were as youngsters in the business, and a whole lot wiser.

Chapter 3
Shorty Slice

Danny Wells was born in Guyana, to a Guyanese father and a mother that was from Belize. He was always tiny; smaller than the average baby, due to being born three weeks premature and spending his first two months in existence at the NICU in the local hospital. He was in an incubator for so long that his dear Mom didn't think that he was strong enough to pull through but his dad knew otherwise. He knew that his son was here for a reason; he was going to be special.

Both of young Shorty Slice's parents were hard-working citizens and they took life seriously. They worked hard and saved harder to provide for their son and give him all of the things that he would ever need or want in his young life. Growing up an only child and being small was very tough, and Danny had to grow up fast or become a statistic of the day-to-day violence in Guyana. In school early on, he had many many fights and was verbally reprimanded on numerous occasions for disruptive conduct, and all of this before he was twelve years old.

It was during his 7th grade year that his parents had decided to take him out of school and move to the United States in order to make a better life for themselves and their son because he was very violent and was always lashing out at anyone that said anything he didn't agree with. Young Danny was eager to move to someplace else, especially the United States.

When they first got to the States, his family came to New Jersey and made their home in Irvington, a suburban city that was a little less violent than Newark and East Orange, its' bigger neighboring cities. His father worked two jobs: during the day he was a cook at a busy diner in Irvington, and at night he worked for parcel service. His mother took care of the house, as well as her child and she also worked as a waitress during the day and on the weekends. She said that the tips were great, and helped them out a lot as a family, so her husband allowed her to continue working there.

It was during his time at Myrtle Avenue Middle School, that he came into his own confidence and asserted himself as not only tough, but a bad little motherfucker. Every time someone teased him about his height or his mixed background, he went upside their heads with a chair or if they were not in a classroom, he would just hit them low then hit them high. That was his element of surprise. He would just punch the shit out of them in the nuts or the stomach, then sock the hell out of them in the face as hard as he could with his little fist. Time after time, he would get suspended from school, and time after time his parents had to come to the school for one thing or another. They labeled him "a little trouble-maker" at middle school, and before his parents knew it, he was in jail before he made it to high school.

One day, after many suspensions during the seventh grade and still managing to excel to the 8th, some dude that wanted to be a thug pushed little Danny down a small flight of stairs, but to the small fellow, it was a "huge" flight of steps. Once little Danny fell, the kid started to call him foreigner and mixed-breed, as well as midget and dwarf. Little Danny reached in his pocket and when his little hand came out, he was flicking open a small but very sharp pocket-knife. Immediately, the bigger kid was scared, but he had fucked with the wrong little gangster today. Little Danny started to run up the eight steps with the knife out, swinging, as the bigger dude tried to frantically kick at his hand or his face. That's where the big punk messed up at, and he realized it as little Danny caught him in the calf with about half of the knife's blade. The big punk yelled out in pain, but little Danny was oblivious to the small crowd that had formed near the top of the doors that led to the staircases. Bystanders watched through the glass at the damage little man from Guyana did to former bully Bruce, as he punch him in the face with the left hand and sliced him up with the knife at the same time, again and again. By the time security came and subdued little Danny Wells, he had damn near killed Bruce Billings, a fifteen-year old eighth grader that was a known bully since he had been in the seventh grade at Myrtle Avenue. When the security was taken him out of the glass doors and down the hallway past all of his peers and classmates handcuffed, a few people started yelling out praises to him and shouting him out.

"Yeah, little man, way to get yours!" someone yelled out.

"Damn little shorty, you did your thing to that big pussy Bruce. It's about time somebody handled his ass!" another kid yelled out to his as he passed them with the guards damn near dragging him by.

"You the man little shorty slice. Don't take no shit from nobody. That's what I'm talking about shorty! And did you see how shorty sliced his big ass up though!" another kid shouted.

"I love you shorty. You are about your business. Big things do come in small packages," some girl yelled out to him. "I will be there for you shorty. I got you. I will be here for you when you get back," she continued to yell out.

He looked back to see a little shorty that use to kick it with him in the classes they had together, her name was Keisha, Keisha Newton. Everybody called her Ki-Ki.

Little Danny didn't care how much damage he had done to the bully, and he was certain he had taught him a valuable lesson in "respecting your peers," and at the same time indirectly gained the respect of the entire school. When they got him to the principals' office, there were police cars and an ambulance out front of the school and the cops were coming to take little Danny away.

He never imagined going to jail or spending any kind of time away from his mom and dad, but when the juvenile judicial court judge slammed the gavel after sentencing him to a five-year term in juvenile prison, the reality had set in and he would have to serve at least three years of the five year sentence.

In the rear of the courtroom, he could hear and see his mother and his new girlfriend Ki-Ki crying their eyes out, wishing that the court did not take him away. Although he had been expelled from school indefinitely, he was still free for a month during his court proceedings, and he and Keisha had hit it off just fine. His mom and dad even let her come over to the house and visit with little Danny because they knew that he would be going away for a while.

He was sent to a training school for boys (a.k.a. "juvenile prison"), in South Jersey, and he would remain there for approximately eight weeks before his first fight and sixty weeks before he caught his first assault charge and made his debut as Shorty Slice.

KARRIEM BILAL MUHAMMAD

It was in the television room, (a little over a year after his first brawl) where young convicts would go to relax and escape the bullshit confines of the dormitory setting and small cottage-like housing units. The individuals who had been there the longest had established "seating arrangements" in the tv room and sometimes when very popular shows were aired or a good "state movie" was offered to the population, the room would be overcrowded and the seats therefore, limited. Young Shorty Slice had gotten moved to a new housing unit when an inmate complained to the c.o. that he had threatened him and another guy in the bathroom, saying that he would rearrange their faces and give them a "permanent tattoo" if they disrespected him in any way.

Now here he was in a new housing unit, sitting in the front row of the television room waiting for Scarface to be shown as the weekend movie. He had prepared his four peanut butter and honey sandwiches (he didn't like jelly because he said it was too much sugar and he was working out) and large Tupperware cup of iced tea and he was ready to go, as was everyone else who was packed into the television room. He forgot to grab his two pillows that he usually sits on when watching tv so he put his Tupperware bowl full of sandwiches and his cup of iced tea on the chair he was sitting in, as an indication to anyone that someone was sitting there. Clearly, with food on the chair one would see that and move on to another available chair if there was one. When Young Shorty Slice came back into the tv room carrying his pillows, he noticed that some bigger dude was sitting in his seat, and not only that, the ignorant motherfucker was sitting there drinking young Shorty Slice's iced tea! He had placed the bowl of sandwiches on the floor, underneath where the television was mounted to the wall.

"Hey man, I was sitting there and my food and drink was left in the seat for a fucking reason!" young Shorty slice said to the dude.

"Get out of my face punk, this is my seat and my iced tea. You didn't know?" voiced the bigger guy, trying to stand up on young Shorty Slice.

"Fuck you bitch!" young Shorty Slice said, as he swung his homemade scalpel downwards across the dudes face, nose, and lips, opening him up instantly.

"Ah!" the big punk screamed as he grabbed his face and tried to rush young Shorty Slice, but he would soon find out why they had called him by that nickname.

"Shut the fuck up nigga. You paid for that seat and iced tea with your ass motherfucker!" yelled young Shorty Slice, as he dodged the dude's advances and cut him several more times in the face, neck, and across the chest.

"Ah! Motherfucker! Ah! Somebody grab this little motherfucker for me. Ah! Ah!" yelled the victim of young Shorty Slice's blade. Just then, some other big dude grabbed young Shorty Slice in the bear hug, rendering him helpless and unable to swing his effective weapon. As the bloody victim rushed at young Shorty Slice, he was kicked in the face by young Shorty Slice's wildly kicking little feet.

"Motherfucker!" screamed the big dude that had grabbed up young Shorty Slice, as he let little Danny go and grabbed at the side of his ribs from a stab wound.

"You two big pussies are not about to jump this little gangster right here. He been handling his fucking business on your man, now you want to fucking flex and jump in. Well flex on me nigga! I got little man's back now chump!" screamed an icepick wielding young Speechless, who didn't even know who little Danny was at this time. He just happened to be in the same jail, in the same dorm, and in the back of the same tv room waiting for Scarface to come on, but he had watched the little kid leave and the bigger bully take his seat and drink his drink. "You faggots been running around here for too long trying to be tough, when you motherfuckers are really pussy, and a G like me been letting you busters live up in here but no more. Both of you motherfuckers have your shit packed the fuck up before these commercials are over nigga!" barked young Speechless at the one he had stabbed, as he swung his icepick at him some more and grabbed young Shorty Slice from the midst.

After the two punks had packed up their property and locker, the officers and brass came and took both young Shorty Slice and young Speechless to the hole in S.H.U. (special housing unit). The big punks had pointed the finger and snitched, and the officers came right in the tv room and grabbed them up, one out the back row and one out of the front row.

During their time in S.H.U. they got familiar with each other's backgrounds and became good friends. Young Kelvin Martin was locked up for four different counts of assault on the young chumps that tried to mug an elderly Italian man. Being that he was half Italian himself, he felt obligated to help the old guy, so he beat the shit out of the four dudes and was later picked up on four counts of second-degree aggravated assault. He said that the old guy reminded him of his grandfather, so he did what he had to do. He was facing eight to sixteen years for the charges, but his high-priced lawyer was provided courtesy of the old man, Salvatore Calzonetti, and he was only sentenced to two-to-four years in juvenile corrections. He was from Newark, born and raised to a black father and Italian mother, and at his young age he was a certified gangster. He called himself Speechless, because he didn't do much talking and the results of what he usually did to people left them "speechless." After young Speechless learned that little Danny was also of mixed race, he expanded the HBH Crew, right there in juvenile prison. Once they had both served ninety days in the box of their one hundred and twenty day S.H.U. terms, they were released and transferred to a more secure facility in Bordentown, New Jersey.

The new jail had a lot more older convicts and inmates there than the other spot in Skillman, New Jersey, and the two HBH Crew members had to do more of the same to establish themselves in the jail. They had the benefit of being placed in the same housing unit after they finished reception together, and they carried it as though they were a team. You couldn't say shit to one without the other getting in your face real quick, and if drama popped off, then they dealt with it together! Up until this point, there were only a few minor incidents where respect had to be established, but those situations were rectified swiftly with HBH Crew violence. You could not get a fair fight where these two were concerned; they were brothers.

For months, and then years, they maintained the flow of exotic weed coming through the facility when everybody else was just bringing in the regular stuff. They ran into beef with the Spanish clique because they were making so much money inside that the Latinos thought that they were slinging heroin but it was just weed. Aside from the regular cliques and groups in the prison system, you had the Crips, Bloods, GD's, VL's, and the righteous regulators, The

Muslims. Then the Latinos had their own barrage of gangs as well: The Latin Kings, Dominican Power, Netas, Trinis, the Mexicans, a Mexican Mafia, and The El Salvadorians, MS13. Just like being in the "free society," with money and violence, comes respect and power.

It was during a basketball game inside the gym one June afternoon, where the Latinos made their move on young Speechless and young Shorty Slice and tried to take them out. Word had spread that the new guys called themselves the HBH Crew, which stood for Half-Breed Hustlers and that they were pushing everything from weed to cocaine to heroin behind the walls of Bordentown, but they were only moving weed.

Little Manny, a known shooter for the Dominicans, walked through the other crews and gangs on a mission. He was gunning for the little one in the HBC Crew called Shorty Slice. There was a price on the both of them but he chose to take the contract on Shorty. His homeboy Chi-Chi from the Latin Kings would be the one to take out this Speechless character.

They approached their targets from both sides of the gym. As they stood near the water fountain talking business, each shooter armed with a jailhouse shank and a bottle of bleach solution to douse into their eyes before stabbing them. As little Manny got closer and closer to the unsuspecting young Shorty Slice, he picked up speed and weaved his way through the crowd until he was tripped by some one that stood amongst a crowd of Spanish cats. Everybody froze as the shank flew in one direction and the small bottle of bleach solution slid across the gymnasium floor in the other direction. Young Speechless immediately snapped into war mode, pulling out an icepick made out of a Phillips head screwdriver he had stolen and smuggled out of Machine Shop vocational. He had a built-in string attached to the weapon and around his wrist so that he could not lose the weapon during battles.

"Get HIM Shorty!" young Speechless told young Shorty Slice, gesturing towards where we had fallen and slid, and turning to scan the gym for any other approaching shooters.

"I got him, come here you motherfucking creep!" said young Shorty Slice, tearing into his face and check, and hands that tried to block his face with two gem star hardback razorblades.

Young Speechless could see someone rushing at him as he fully turned around and he just reacted. He brought up his left arm to absorb the impact of the weapon that Chi-Chi swung at his head, catching the small metal blade in his muscular forearm. He then swung his own icepick upwards twice towards Chi-Chi's lung, then his armpit.

"*Aye conyo*! Motherfucker! Ah he poked me! Motherfucker take this!" an injured Chi-Chi screamed out loud amongst all the noise and chaos, as he attempted to throw the bleach into the face of young Speechless. Young Speechless saw the move and anticipated it. He ducked just in time and with his injured arm he pushed Chi-Chi backwards until he was off balance, then he rushed him, stabbing him three more times before the guards rushed in and subdued everyone involved. Young Shorty Slice was knocked out by the guards that tried to interfere in what he was doing on the floor to little Manny that as sent by DP. There was blood everywhere in that area of the gym, and the officers were slipping and sliding as they tried to break up the assault, and one of them was cut deeply on the hand by one of Shorty Slice's razors. They beat his little ass unconscious and threw him and his partner in the SHU when they got out of the institutions infirmary. As the officers were bringing little Manny by a group of officers on his way to the outside hospital, he turned towards a young Puerto Rican dude with his hair slicked back and down into a really long braid that ran down his back and said,

"I know that was YOU that tripped me motherfucker, you are going to pay for that shit Pretty Boy bitch!" hissed an infuriated little Manny through clenched teeth at the slick-haired youth.

"Fuck you bitch, it's whatever, whenever, wherever faggot!" replied the kid that had tripped little Manny.

After 180 days in the Administrative Segregation Unit (long-term keep lock), young Speechless and young Shorty Slice was released back into population and resumed business as usual. The only exception was that little Manny had signed in Protective Custody behind some drama he had with some half-Dominican/half Puerto Rican kid everybody called Pretty Boy from North Newark. After little Manny was released from the hospital and had healed up, he sought out revenge for being tripped during the assassination attempt on the

HBH Crew in the gym, and he knew that it was Pretty Boy who had tripped him. He tried to bring the noise to young Pretty Boy, but to no avail because young Pretty Boy was a thorough and official dude. Young Pretty Boy whipped little Manny's ass, then told him to go get a weapon because his "hand skills" weren't good enough for fighting a G like him. Then he whooped little Manny's ass again a day later when he came back with a shank after he took it from him and passed it to one of his boys from the North Newark.

Once the knife was out of the equation, young Pretty Boy beat the shit out of little Manny, then ripped his face open with a gem star razor. Little Manny was humiliated after that and he had pressure on him from Dominican Power ever since the failed attempt on the HBH Crew in the gym months ago so he signed into P.C. and got shipped out of the jail to another spot further South. The Dominicans or the Latin Kings didn't try to come at the HBH Crew anymore because they had a mutual respect for gangsters. And besides that, word had spread that Pretty Boy from North Newark was looking to link up with them and everyone in the joint respected young Pretty Boy out of respect for his father and family's reputation in the game. Plus, young Pretty Boy was fucking ruthless!

Everyone was in the yard that was anyone in the jail on this particular day, and young Speechless and young Shorty Slice was over to the side of the main yard flow smoking top notch weed out of cigars, while everyone else fought and scrounged for little skinny "spider web" joints, which were unbelievably scrawny and skinny, mostly paper, and sold for two packs of cigarettes per joint of smoke. They sat and talked about the plans they had to take over the entire city of Newark and then some when they got out, and they talked about the women that were holding them down while they did their time in jail. Young Shorty Slice still had Ki-Ki riding with him like a trooper, and young Speechless had a few females coming in bringing that package to keep their business running consistently. They were in the middle of their conversation when, all of a sudden three Latino guys approached them. Just when young Shorty Slice was reaching for his weapon, the kid with the long braid told the other two dudes to fall back and wait for him a few feet away from where the guys were talking.

"What's up brothers? I came to talk business, no need for the steel. I come in peace," said young Pretty Boy.

"Who are you?" asked young Shorty Slice being cautious, his hand still under his sweatshirt and on his shank.

"Pretty Boy from North Newark," he said extending his hand to the both of them for a handshake. "I heard a lot about you guys and I think we can do business; I think we should be a team!" he continued.

"We are already a team. We are an exceptional team, and we are not excepting applications bro," spoke young Speechless.

"This is not an application bro, this is an interview. You see, I am half Dominican and half Puerto Rican, and I believe the HBH Crew is where I belong," said young Pretty Boy.

"Interview huh? How do you know about HBH anyway? You are real confident my man. My name is Speechless, and this is Shorty Slice," young Speechless said as they shook Pretty Boy's hand.

"Yeah, confidence is one of my qualities amigo and I know about you through Chinky. We grew up together, I gave him that nickname," said young Pretty Boy.

"I remember hearing that you took care of that pussy little Manny from DP. Made him sign into PC and everything!" remarked young Shorty Slice.

"Hell yeah man, fuck that bitch ass nigga. I peeped him trying to get the drop on you in the gym that day, and I tripped his ass hoping that would slow him down and it did!" responded young Pretty Boy.

"It most certainly did slow him down, that was YOU? You helped out a lot bro, and gave us the time we needed to handle our business and if you are cool with Chinky then you are family!" spoke young Speechless.

"It was nothing bro. I was trying to fuck with your team back then, but then you two went to the box and the process was held up but here we are now, what's good?" asked young Pretty Boy.

"Walk with us for the rest of the yard period brother, and if those are your shooters, they can fall back right now. You don't need them, you are with us," said young Speechless.

"Right, I will tell them to fall back and play the handball court until the yard go-back is that cool?" asked young Pretty Boy.

"That's cool," responded young Speechless.

SWITCH HITTER 2: 50/50 Crew: 'Til Death Do Us

They walked the yard and talked about the criteria, the loyalty, and the future aspirations of the HBH Crew; what the crew stood for and wouldn't stand for. That was the day that the crew expanded, and they were always together until they were all released a year later. Young Speechless was released in January, young Pretty Boy was released in May, and young Shorty Slice came home in September.

Chapter 4
The Unbreakable Bond

When Chinky was discovered by Speechless' half-brother, Tito Calversero and his two-man team, he was in really bad shape. He had almost died due to the tremendous amount of blood he had lost. Immediately, Tito called Speechless and told him that they had Chinky and that he would be taken to the doctor ASAP and be taken care of.

Tito and his crew had pulled up at the rear entrance to the doctors' mansion, and quickly got him inside. Doctor Abdullah had already been called in advance so he was ready for them when they pulled up, and once inside, he swiftly went to work on Chinky's three bullets wounds. He had gotten Chinky's blood type from Speechless over the phone and therefore was able to give Chinky the necessary transfusion he needed to save his life. The good doctor had everything, and his humongous basement was like a miniature emergency room. He assured his good friend Mr. Calversero, that his friend would indeed live to see better days.

Speechless and Gorilla got to Miami about two hours after they had talked to Tito when they had found Chinky. It took them another twenty-five minutes to get to the secluded area where the doctor resided, and they were excited that their brother was still alive.

"Brother! It's so good to see you. It has been a long time!" said Tito, as he hugged Speechless.

"Yeah bro, I know it has been a long time for sure. Thank you for everything you've done to make sure one of mines was safe. Sorry about the old man too, he was the best," Speechless said to Tito as he handed him the duffel bag full of cash. Tito then passed the bag to Marko, who took it outside to the Audi A7 and put the money in the trunk.

"This here is our other brother Gorilla. Gorilla this is Tito Calversero, this is family," Speechless said as he introduced them, Tito still not believing how big Gorilla was at six foot eight and three hundred and ninety pounds, but recognizing that the name was a fitting one.

"Very well. These are my right and left hands, Marko, and Tony, also family," Tito said introducing everyone.

Tito had paid the doctor one hundred and fifty thousand dollars for his services, and when Speechless brought Tito his million dollars, Speechless also gave the doctor an additional hundred thousand dollars and thanked him for helping out and saving his brothers' life on such short notice. They were happy as hell to see Slanted-Eyes still alive after hearing that he had lost so much blood. The two of them approached his bedside together and just looked down at their warrior, brother, and swore revenge against those responsible.

"That motherfucker baby Hatchet is a fucking dead man and those Pocahontas Mamas are some dead bitches too!" spoke Gorilla.

"I know brother, this shit cannot go unanswered in the least and as soon as Chinky opens up his motherfucking eyes you need to be out there looking for this motherfucker Gorilla, for real," Speechless said.

"Say no more bro, I am on it!" barked Gorilla.

"I have eyes and ears all over this part of the fucking state, so if you guys need anything, do not hesitate to ask. You guys are family," said Tito.

"He is still slightly comatose but all vitals show that he will pull through just fine once he wakes up," said Doctor Amin Abdullah.

"Thanks for everything Doc, we really appreciate all that you've done but I am going to need my brother to rest up here for as long as it takes because we don't want to cause any more damage by moving him. We will take him home when he can stand, if that's alright with you," commented Speechless, as he shook the Doctors' hand.

"Take as long as you need. My basement is like a condo as you can see, very comfortable," said the good doctor. "Besides, Salvatore was one of my best friends and his sons are like my nephews, understand?" he concluded, giving Speechless a stern look.

"Understood Doc," replied Speechless.

"Understood," responded Gorilla.

"Absolutely understood Doctor Abdullah," said Tito.

"How long does it usually take someone to recover from injuries this severe Doc?" Speechless asked.

"Sometimes weeks, sometimes months, but he will be fine. He is in good hands now," said Doctor Abdullah.

Speechless and Gorilla did some shopping and temporarily moved down to Miami, Florida, making the best of Doctor Abdullah's basement/condo for two ½ weeks until Chinky opened up his eyes as they were approaching the 3rd week of his coma.

"Guys come in here, he's awake! Chinky is awake! His eyes are open!" yelled Gorilla, who had been sitting with Chinky for a few hours.

"Oh shit!" yelled Speechless rushing into the recovery room that Chinky was recuperating in. "Chinky it's about damn time soldier. You had your brothers worried to death man!" continued Speechless, smiling from ear-to-ear and shaking Chinky's hand. Then he called Shorty Slice and Pretty Boy to tell them the great news!

Tito, Marko, and Tony walked in and shook Chinky's hand as well, and they also offered their best wishes and congratulations to him.

"Brother, these are the gangsters that saved your life bro. When we were damn near three hours away from you, these three were the ones that answered the call and located you for us. Then me and Gorilla flew down as soon as the jet was ready.

With his eyes wide open and blinking slowly, Chinky focused on everyone around him and said five simple words.

"Thanks. Baby Hatchet got away."

In about a week after he had opened his eyes, Chinky was up and running, literally. He walked all around Dr. Abdullah's mansion on a regular basis and ran on the treadmill at least twice a day. He weight-trained with only light weights and increased his reps, as to not deprive himself of the proper "burn" when he worked-out and although he lost a tremendous about of blood, the wounds he suffered did not do any muscle or tendon damage. Other than the scars he had to remind him and some weight loss, he was back to himself, and as strong as an ox! He and Speechless were out looking around for any signs or word on Baby Hatchet; so was Gorilla on another side of town. And also there was Tito, with his two-man team on the opposite side of the city.

The infamous strip club Ballers & Broads, popular known as

"B&B's" was now closed down and there were some signs up for plans on new developments coming soon. As they drove past it and Chinky brought Speechless up to date on some of the events that took place inside the club that night, he also showed him the enormous parking garage he had taken refuge in when he was dying.

"Thank God you knew people down here bro, otherwise my ass would have been dead and stinking in that rental car Speechless, and not only people but good people, you know what I'm saying," said Chinky.

"Thank God for family!" responded Speechless. "I would have done the same thing for him if Marko or Tony was wounded and dying in New Jersey after a mission or a gunfight!" he continued to explain.

"I know bro, I know you, and that's just how you are. Hell, that's how we all are loyal!" returned Chinky. "I owe you all my life bro, thanks," concluded Chinky.

"You're welcome and you don't owe any of us any motherfucking thing Slanted-Eyes. You've already given us your life, time and time again brother," Speechless said, as he continued to drive the Mercedes S550, praying that they would see Baby Hatchet, but knowing it was a far-fetched thought.

Tito, Marko, and Tony cruised the streets of Westside of Miami in a cranberry Range Rover HSE looking for any signs of Baby Hatchet or anyone that they could possibly squeeze for information about baby Hatchet's whereabouts. Between the three of them, they knew a lot of people all over the state of Florida but especially Miami. Both Marko and Tony were from Miami, born and raised, even though they dibbled and dabbled back and forth to New York and New Jersey since they were young gangsters coming up. Now they were grown killers, and ultimately loyal to Tito, their boss and big brother, who taught them right and made them millionaires. They had known Tito Calversero ever since they were nineteen years old and attending technical educational school and Tito was 24, already one of the toughest "quiet guys" they had ever met, and he got nothing but respect from people. He didn't make much noise, but when he moved, motherfuckers disappeared and was never heard of again.

They drove around for about an hour before Marko spotted Timmy

Falcone a.k.a. "Timmy Tell-it-all," also referred to as "Timmy Talk-a-lot." He had been spreading gossip and telling peoples business ever since junior high school, and as he got older, he got worse. No matter how many threats or ass-whippings he would receive for talking too much, he just wouldn't shut the fuck up! Immediately Marko pulled the vehicle over and hopped out, with Tony right with him and Tito observing from the truck. They approached Timmy and he didn't dare try to run or flee in any way from them, he knew better than that. They questioned him for ten minutes, and from that ten minutes, they learned that this Baby Hatchet character was allegedly the ringleader of this new clique of gangsters running around crazy and getting all kinds of money all over Miami. They were called The Terribles, and supposedly, word on the street is that was an accurate description of how they were, terrible! They thanked Timmy Tell-it-all, and gave him five hundred dollars for the valuable information, only half of what they were offering for anyone's info leading to Baby Hatchet. Marko couldn't stand the likes of Timmy.

    The Terribles were now getting to be known all over Miami fast, but their main geographical part of the city to be comfortable in was the Westside of Miami, close to the beach. They had made that part of Miami their home, their headquarters. Tito, being the Don that he was, would start at the head of any family or gang, or clique, and question them in a sit down because that's just how he was and if you showed disrespect, he had you killed. He offered the leaders of the gangs each fifty-thousand dollars for their time and information and found out more and more from each group once the leaders squeezed the crew because no one liked The Terribles at all. They didn't discriminate when it came to enemies or victims, they went at anyone, anywhere! When they regrouped later on that day, information was shared between themselves and the 50/50 Crew about Baby Hatchet and his new "reborn" Butcher Boys crew, now going by, "The Terribles." Word on the street also, was that The Terribles ran closely with this female clique of dime pieces that went by "Diamond Dolls," and were the younger sisters and cousins of all the Pocahontas Mamas that had died in the massacre at B&B's strip club. They were just as devious and deadly as their predecessors and they were out for vengeance at any cost. Mostly all of the Diamond Dolls were "booed-up" with someone out of The Terribles clique, but these ruthless young bitches still did them because they knew the value of "pussy power," so they didn't let anyone control them; they did the controlling.

"So you mean to tell me, that not only did this punk motherfucker survive, but that he has put together a new crew that are even worst that that of the Butcher Bums back in Jersey?" asked Speechless, directing his question at Tito.

"These motherfuckers ALL are going to die when it's all over with! Fuck all of 'em and those little bitches too, because their sisters killed Twin and Uzi Malik, who just so happen to save my motherfucking life!" yelled Chinky. "Whatever the fuck it takes, however long it lasts, I want that motherfucker more than anyone!" he continued, as he slammed his fist down on the table they all sat at.

"This shit will not go unanswered brother, you already know that shit. For our fallen brothers and for Dolly, these bastards are all going to fall until we get Baby Hatchet's pussy ass," said Gorilla, speaking up and asserting himself in the plan to track their target down. "I am personally going to put that work in. This motherfucker has touched too many members of this family! He's in the history books!" barked Gorilla mad as hell.

"He is doing a lot of things down here my friends, and he has been for a little while now. His connection to the white is serious, and he has branched-out very fast. He was smart to use this Cynthia bitch to get around and make his moves, because she is the younger sister of the Cubans that supply this faggot!" explained Tito. "All of the information we have acquired, I consider useful and accurate, and we should act on it as soon as possible!" concluded Tito.

"Give me a copy of those known spots and areas Tito, I got to get the fuck out of here and track this pussy down!" said Gorilla. Tito handed him a copy, then he handed everyone else a copy as Gorilla stood up to excuse himself, dap his family, and then he left after gripping up.

"Now there's a man on a mission right there, he's not even waiting for back-up, a soldier," said Marko.

"Yeah he is in true Gorilla-mode right now, focused!" remarked Tony.

"We are all brothers in the 50/50 Crew, but Chinky and Gorilla are like fraternal twins, and they were super-tight from day one; always hanging out, working-out, or double-dating with their girlfriends Jamaica and Dolly. Rest in Peace Dolly. They are also the only two of the crew never to see a jail cell or even get booked on a charge. They move alike," Speechless said.

"That's my big brother, just like Speechless and Shorty Slice are my big brothers too. Gorilla is just over-protective of me, and he's been that way ever since I saved his life once years ago," Chinky said. "He probably wishes he was down here with us all when that shit went popped off with Baby Hatchet at the strip club, but that was my call. I took on that assignment and the responsibility that comes along with it by myself. Shit just got out of hand and all crazy. We did not anticipate this motherfucker getting any assistance from those Indian bitches. They got the drop on Uzi Malik and Twin, and Dolly lost her life that night as well," Chinky continued.

"Don't worry about that, you guys are family and now you have allies in this war!" spoke Tito.

"Thank you Tito, Marko, and Tony. We really appreciate all the help guys, we are already making progress. Now it's time to track this motherfucker down!" expressed Speechless.

Chapter 5
Chinky

Johnny Chow was the name he was given at birth by his mother, but he would soon shed away any "normal" parts of his life and branch-out to do his own thing at a very young age. His father, a Puerto Rican hustler/gangster from North Newark, New Jersey had met his mother when he was oversees doing a tour of duty. His mother, Joan Chow, was a proud bartender and made a pretty lucrative living whenever the bar she worked at was busy and it was always thriving with sailors, soldiers, and troublemakers.

She was very beautiful and could have easily been a model of clothes or cosmetics but she chose at a very young age to become a bartender because the demand was so great for one. All of the male bartenders would either get into arguments, fights, or even get killed for sleeping with someone else's woman. She had the personality to go along with the position so after she was shown the ropes of what to do and got past all of the harassment, she was able to excel as a full-fledged bartender. From the age of sixteen years old, she had been working in the Flaming Dragon, a local bar and grill and at the age of twenty, she met her dream come true in the form of an American soldier.

Jonathan "Jo-Jo" Martinez was doing a tour in Korea for the United States Marines and after the mission, he and his detail had chosen to relax and take a load off of their feet in a small but thriving village. One of his comrades had secured a couple of rooms at a hotel/rooming house for the guys and after they settled in, they had decided to go and have a few drinks before heading back home to the states in a few days.

While he was at the bar, Jo-Jo was transfixed on the Asian female bartender that was serving drinks and having conversations so effortlessly with everyone that she came in contact with. She had eyes that were amazing and a smile had lit up the poorly lit tavern every time her lips separated. As she served one particular fellow, all of a sudden her pretty smile turned into a frown and she shook her head no. The guy then lurched forward as she attempted to back up and he grabbed her by the forearms to pull her closer to him forcing her to talk to him. Jo-Jo was raised up to protect and respect women so he felt obligated to help the pretty young Asian lady in distress. He quickly walked over to the hooligan and told him to release his woman immediately and leave the bar or be dealt with. The harasser turned around to see where the voice was coming from and was met by a menacing stare from Jo-Jo.

"Who in thee fuck are you?" asked the drunken thug.

"I just told you who I was. I'm her motherfucking man! Now you don't have any more seconds, you should have left when I said so!" barked Jo-Jo. With that said, Jo-Jo Martinez broke the man down with a punch to the spine, then a left hook to the man's head, followed by a vicious knee to the face as the man descended to the floor. When the man's friends attempted to come to his rescue, they were confronted and then surrounded by Jo-Jo's armed comrades.

"Trust me, you all don't want these motherfucking problems right here," Jo-Jo reminded them, as they stopped in their tracks, and picked up their battered man then left.

Joan and Jo-Jo saw each other almost every day after that initial encounter at the bar and they spent almost every single night together. She told him how she wanted to escape the jungles of the East and travel to the United States to make a better life for herself. She told him that she was fed up with the harassment that comes with the job from time to time and that she had experienced this treatment her entire life. Two weeks later after a whirlwind romance and on the day of his departure to the states, she told him that she was pregnant and that she was having the baby no matter what. Three months after that, while she was four months pregnant, they were married and she was a citizen of the United States.

They made their home in Newark, New Jersey near Park Avenue and Branch Brook Park, on the north side. After his tour of duty, Jo-Jo hooked up with a few old partners of his and started selling heavy drugs in the North Newark area. He was arrested twice while hustling: once for aggravated assault and once for drug possession, to which he pled out to and got sentenced to probation and a drug program. His defense in the drug case was that he was a drug user, NOT drug dealer. They gave him a 6-month residential drug program and two years of probation for the charge.

Once he was home from the drug case, he turned things up in the streets with his team and excelled tremendously by killing off the competition and kidnapping rivals for substantial amounts of ransom money from time to time. He became a notorious man in the streets of North Newark and his reputation followed him all over Essex County. He ran with the Gonzalez crew and they were very well respected abroad in that area. They owned everything from bodegas to record stores and restaurants. They had territories as opposed to blocks, and within their territories, no one sold anything but them!

As Jo-Jo Martinez and the Gonzalez family grew in success over the years, the offspring of Ricardo Gonzalez Sr. and Jonathan "Jo-Jo" Martinez were growing up together in the same hood of North Newark. They had been friends since they were four years old at the same daycare.

Both young Chinky and young Pretty Boy were spoiled kids because their dads were official hustlers and true gangsters so no one fucked with them. Plus, they were financially well-off. They were bad as shit in elementary school, and young Chinky always beat up people for teasing him. Young Pretty Boy was just always there when shit jumped off and made sure that it was finished. They both started smoking weed at eleven years old. That's when young Pretty Boy nicknamed little Johnny "Chinky" and by the time they were starting middle school, young Pretty Boy was on his way to juvenile prison for slashing two brothers in the face after they tried to jump him in the gym in between classes.

Young Pretty Boy was cutting through the gym as most kids did in between classes, when Jimmy and his younger brother Jonah Clark tried to do him harm being that he didn't have the young Chinese cat with him (so they thought). As soon as Jimmy snuffed young Pretty Boy from the blindside, before his brother had a chance to get a lick in, young Pretty Boy had reached into the folder he was carrying and pulled out a fluorescent orange box cutter and stared slashing faces like a professional knife handler. The more they blocked the attacks, the faster he sliced their faces and by the time the security guards arrived, each of them had five to six slashes somewhere on their face. Young Pretty Boy was only twelve years old at the time.

When young Pretty Boy went to jail, young Chinky lost his best friend for a couple of years, and the Clark brothers lost a father forever. Mr. James Martin Clark was found badly beaten and shot once in the back of the head behind the dumpster of a local bar he frequented. His family had his body cremated out of fear that his funeral could be shot up by members of the Gonzalez organization. After that, his widow and sons moved away somewhere out West.

Young Chinky started fucking with the streets two years after his brother went away to do his time. He was dating heavy and doing what he had to do to keep his mind off of his loss. He was traveling out of the North Newark area on a regular basis seeing different females in different areas of Newark, always carrying his twenty-five automatic and at least four blunts of smoke already rolled up. He always thought that if you stopped somewhere to roll up, then somebody could roll up on and rob you, or even kill you so he was never caught slipping.

He was in the Vailsburg section visiting this cutie when she wanted him to pick up some wings and fries from the Chinese take-out on his way to her house. He got off the number eighteen bus and went into the restaurant, which was right around the corner from her house. There was only one guy in from of him ordering food, and as soon as he was done he stepped to the side so that young Chinky could order. As soon as young Chinky was getting ready to order his shorty's food, three more guys came into the spot acting rowdy and being disrespectful towards the oriental people behind the glass, then one of them noticed that Asian as well.

"Yo Jackie Chan nephew! Hurry up so me and my partners can eat motherfucker!" barked the rude cat that had two of his boys with him.

Young Chinky turned around to look at the person that was talking and saw that there were three of them, then he turned to the guy waiting for his food and asked him,

"Are they with you man?" he asked the tall cat that had ordered before him.

"Negative, do you-" replied young Speechless. Then without even finishing the rest of his order, young Chinky turned around with the small pistol in his hand and murder on his mind.

"I should shoot you in the motherfucking forehead and make your eyes touch bitch, but being that you are a dick-less coward, I'm going to leave you," POW! (the gun fired) "like I found you pussy!" young Chinky told him as he squeezed the trigger once shooting him in the pelvis area. His friends immediately hauled ass up out of the Chinese spot as the gunshot echoed in the small confinement, driving the people behind the counter frantic.

He turned and made eye contact with young Speechless and said two words,

"Thanks man." And then he walked out of the store with his gun in his pocket, and no Chinese food.

Three weeks later, young Speechless was posted up on one of his blocks when he saw a female that never fucked with anyone from the neighborhood, leaving her apartment with the same young Chinese cat he had seen pop the shit out of some clown up in Ivy Hill. He had to get this niggas attention.

"Brother man, can I get a minute? We need to talk," young Speechless yelled as he got closer to the couple.

"You know him?" she asked young Chinky.

"No, but I recognize him. Relax baby, I don't think there is going to be trouble alright," said young Chinky to the girl Wanda he was seeing down the hill near Clinton and Bergen.

"If you don't mind Wanda, I would like to talk with brother man privately. Would you please excuse us? I promise that I will not keep him away from you too long," young Speechless said as he walked up on them.

"No problem, Kelvin," replied Wanda.

She went back in the house as young Speechless introduced himself to young Chinky and explained to him his vision. He figured that young Chinky was Chinese and black because he damn sure carried himself and held his own, like a black person in the streets would. Therefore, he would be the very first recruit for the HBH Crew. He laid the whole shit out for him concisely as they walked and talked; the plans and the aspirations of long-term success in the streets. He talked about obtaining millions a piece, each one of his crew rich beyond their dreams. He explained that there would be much bloodshed in their climb to success, but promised to be on the frontline of every single motherfucking war that they went through in life.

They exchanged information and met up the next day to open up shop in areas surrounding North Newark because that was closer to young Chinky's home turf. Besides, young Speechless already had money down BT, Bradley's Courts, Isabella & 18th Ave., Clinton Avenue and Bergen, and South Orange Avenue & Littleton. The sooner he expanded his crew, the more areas they could conquer and the richer they will be.

He and Chinky were getting money! They had twenty workers scattered about the different locations young Speechless had product moving, and they were on the rise with a bigger and better connection for the work they pushed. Prices would be guaranteed cheaper and 15% better quality! He was shocked to find out that young Chinky was mixed with Korean and Puerto Rican, but by the way he moved you could tell he wasn't just Asian. He had the streets of Newark embedded in him at an early age and was brought up around Puerto Ricans, Dominicans, and Blacks that hustled all day long.

For a year straight they climbed and stacked, stacked and climbed the ladder of the underworld. Then, just when they were at the beginning of something prosperous and good, young Speechless had to go away and do time for some assault charges that he had pending and he would be gone for two-to-four years.

In his absence, young Chinky took over temporarily and ran things with the help of a lot of shooters who were loyal to young Speechless and grateful for his generosity. He maintained the areas they ran product out of, and kept the workers loyal by giving them 50% of their packages and paying for the small cars they rode around in hustling. Every now and then, he would have to send the shooters somewhere to regulate something when outsiders tried to take over the turf. In North Newark, he was widely known and respected as "Jo-Jo's son but in the other sections of Newark, Ironbound, Weequahic, Down the Hill, Ivy Hill, and Newark's neighbor, Irvington, he would have to earn the respect that was expected. One thing he had against him was that he was a Chinese looking cat in a hood of Blacks, Puerto Ricans, and middle-class whites making money and the other thing he had against him was that he was young.

There were a few older gangsters in the neighborhoods that just couldn't resist trying young Chinky and testing his gangster because he had people making money on blocks they had grew up on! During the first year of young Speechless' incarceration, twenty people got shot at the order of young Chinky, four of them killed, the others just warned not to fuck with the young Asian cat that was HBH. He always rode around in cars with bullet-proof windows and always had an older female driving him around because he kept a gun on him, always!

All of the cars he was driven around in were all white: A white Benz S500 coupe, a white convertible 325i BMW, a white Jetta with white & chrome 5-star rims, and a white Jeep Cherokee with white BBS rims on it. He had all of the copies to the keys that young Speechless owned with the exception of the safe deposit boxes that were his, courtesy of his mentor Salvatore. He had access to most of his money and jewelry, as well as his vehicles, but he was as loyal as they come and he would never betray a friend. His status increased and so did his popularity in the streets, but he kept his focus on his two brothers that were locked up: Pretty Boy, his childhood blood brother and Speechless, the leader of his crew.

By the time young Chinky was sixteen, his people were getting ready to come home from jail and he was maintaining things as usual. It had been three years.

He never went to visit young Pretty Boy because in the beginning of his stretch, young Pretty Boy was always in lock-up for fighting or assaulting someone so he didn't want to receive any visits looking through a glass at his family. He had chosen to tough it out until he got established in whatever population that they put him in. All young Pretty Boy needed were females coming to see him and bringing him drugs to sell so he could be comfortable, and still feel human, hustling and shining behind the wall. Young Chinky didn't visit young Speechless because he didn't need to. Young Speechless told him that he was more important to the organization in the streets and all he had to worry about was getting chicks up there every single weekend to see his comrade and make sure the packages kept coming, and they did. Between the mules, they had broken down and sold a pound every month. Half a pound of good every two weeks, and that is tremendously great for steady volume in a jail and they did this for a least a solid year straight. They only fucked with people that had straight up cash or sent the money to the designated address first before they got their drugs. Credit only caused problems and they were not in the "problem business," they were in the money business and preparing to take over Newark when they touched down.

Two weeks before young Speechless was scheduled to get out of jail, young Chinky was shot at and his young girlfriend hurt badly from a gunshot wound to the neck while they were leaving the movies out in Amboy. The girl eventually survived, but the shooters didn't. They were tracked down and dealt with severely. They were locals from Newark that followed young Chinky's driver. The driver survived as well. He was strapped with a bullet-proof vest and armed with a Beretta when the shoot-out took place, and he was able to protect young Chinky when he had shot one of the perpetrators as they fled.

The homecoming for young Speechless was huge and the news of the HBH Crew getting two new brothers was tremendous news to young Chinky. Especially when he found out that his own blood brother Pretty Boy was on the team, and was going to be part of the family.

Chapter 6
The Terribles

When Baby Hatchet had decided to put together his family of goons and take over part of Miami, he didn't do it alone. He had the connections of Ms. Cuba and her brothers, who were the Cuban cocaine suppliers that kept them in business. He knew that shit would get crazy with all of the crews and gangs in Miami, so he used the same recipe that his brother Hatchet had used when he formed the Butcher Boys up in Irvington, New Jersey. He gathered the craziest motherfuckers he could get his hands on and he drilled home the fact that violence ruled in any area, any town, in any state. The Cuban connection wanted swift retribution for the death of their sister, and at any cost! They had pressure on Baby Hatchet and The Terribles to produce results and execute vengeance on those responsible for their baby sisters' horrible death.

The Terribles ran around reckless even though they were almost rich in the drug game. It was their attitudes and total disregard for human life that made them "terrible." They didn't give a fuck who you were or what you claimed. If they felt they could get away with it then you were dead, dead, dead. The leader of The Terribles was twenty-four-year-old Paco. He was a ruthless Puerto Rican that was raised in Little Havana by some Cuban gangsters since he was ten years old.

Their second in command was Tattoo, who was a twenty-one-year-old full-blooded Cuban and was also brought up in Little Havana. Tattoo was a fool, and didn't care about shit since being abandoned when he was five years old. He got the nickname because of the one hundred tattoos he had all over his body, from neck to calf. The captain of The Terribles was an eighteen year old Dominican cat named Mohawk, who had pledged his loyalty to the gang by getting "Terrible" tattooed on both sides of his Mohawk–style haircut. The lieutenant of The Terribles was the Money Moe, who was the younger brother of Paco and he was just as ruthless and reckless as his older brother.

Money Moe was only eighteen years old, but he had a mentality like a 30-year-old hustler. They had all been employed by Baby Hatchet and Ms. Cuba for two years now, and it was time to advance. Promotions were promised to those responsible for the capture or murder of the people responsible for Ms. Cuba's death and retribution was promised by her brothers if no one was brought to justice. Since the massacre at B&B'S strip club, bodies were dropping all over Miami in response to the loss of one of their leaders, and messages were sent in blood. They hit ever crew that was known to be getting money in that particular area of Miami, and the murders were piling up. The Terribles were at least ninety members deep, and they were spread out abroad in ten different areas of Miami making drug money, extorting stores that weren't on their payroll, and terrorizing neighborhoods. They knew all about the history of the Butcher Boys crew from New Jersey that was annihilated by the 50/50 Crew, and they knew that they were the extension of The Butcher Boys; the new wave of terror in the streets.

Eventually, they had plans to increase their size and gradually migrate back into northern New Jersey and reclaim their turf and then some, but those plans were set back tremendously when Ms. Cuba was murdered along with several of the Pocahontas Mamas and a few of Baby Hatchet's bodyguards. The Terribles had pressure on them from two different angles to bring forth justice for the slaughter at the strip club; on one side, you had the brothers of Ms. Cuba (the connect) pressuring them, and on the other hand, you had the younger sisters of the slain Pocahontas Mamas pressuring them as well.

After all, they were the boyfriends of the "Diamond Dolls," who were the little sisters of: Diamond, Topaz, Gemma, and the Twins (Ruby & Sapphire) who all died in the shootout at B&B's. The only one of the Pocahontas Mamas that had survived the slaughter was Emerald, but she had been stabbed in her spine and neck with an icepick by Chinky, so she was crippled and wheelchair bound for the rest of her life. Her little sister was Turquoise, captain of the Diamond Dolls, and one evil little bad bitch. She always used her natural teal-green eyes to lure potential victims; drug dealers, and ball players and once she had them in her company, they were either robbed, killed, or extorted. Just like the rest of the Diamond Dolls, she wanted revenge for her big sister and she wouldn't rest until retribution was carried out!

Since they had access to an unlimited supply of the purest cocaine, they didn't worry about anything where the drug game was concerned, because they could out-do any competition, and if they couldn't compete then they just killed you if they could get away with it. All of the top ranked members of The Terribles had at least one murder under his belt, whether they did it for initiation into the gang or committed it in the course of hustling. All the members with status also drove only orange-colored cars representing the state of Florida. Every other member drove only vehicles that were yellow, meaning that they had yet to earn stripes; they were just dealers, shooters, or both. Still, all of the cars that belonged to members of The Terribles were chromed-out and detailed to look like show cars, so even the soldiers were proud to be shining as they drove around representing their team.

"We are out there every day looking for these motherfuckers Paco, day and night, looking for any answers to Ms. Cuba's murder," Tattoo said to his leader.

"I don't care what it takes bro, we have to make something happen soon or else these Cuban motherfuckers are going to start taking us out one by one until they feel that their sister is avenged!" Paco yelled. "We have worked too damn hard to be removed from our positions just because we can't find some people! Find them!" he continued to scream.

"Shit is not as easy as it sounds Paco. We really are doing all we can out there in them streets to solve this problem. We are everywhere out there," remarked Mohawk. "I have some people on the east searching as well for anyone with information on these fuckers from up Jersey," he continued.

"Well search harder, look further, pay more ransom, whatever the fuck you have to do to get shit done, do it!" Paco concluded.

Meanwhile, Baby Hatchet was at an exclusive hospital in Orlando which had a recovery ward that catered to high-profile sports figures, celebrities, and big-time drug dealers. He had shelled-out a million dollars to be treated and stashed away at the facility until he was completely healed up from his injures, and the only two people he was in contact with was Paco, leader of his Terribles clique, and Ramon who was Ms. Cuba's oldest brother, and the head of their cocaine connection. Ramon had made it perfectly clear to Baby Hatchet that if his sisters' killers were not brought to street justice, then not only would their sweet cocaine supply be over and done with, but so would his existence. Baby Hatchet just nodded his head, as if he understood the consequences. He called Paco and had learned that they had gotten nowhere with the search for any signs of the 50/50 Crew down in Florida, and it was as if the half Chinese motherfucker just disappeared from the scene that night at Ballers & Broads strip club.

"Well we have do something fast because these motherfuckers are not playing any motherfucking games Paco, and I am not ready for this shit to end yet, you feel me? We are just getting started out here, the last thing we need is to lose our connection or go to fucking war with them," Baby Hatchet said to Paco.

"I know B.H. We have got to increase our surveillance and men in the streets until we get the whereabouts of this 50/50 Crew, especially the Chinese one that killed Ms. Cuba!" replied Paco.

"Then get that shit done already!" yelled Baby Hatchet into the phone receiver.

It took a few weeks to get any information on the 50/50 Crew, but Paco was successful due to his female acquaintances he had up in New Jersey and New York. He had female relatives or mistresses in almost every hair salon in every city within Essex County, and across the water in New York City. It was only a matter of time.

He had been told by his cousin Rosetta, that the sister of Pretty Boy, one of the top members of the 50/50 Crew, was getting married to his right-hand man/enforcer ,Diablo, and that they would be honeymooning in South Beach, Miami Florida in a couple of months. She said that she didn't know where the wedding would be, but that she heard it would be a destination wedding with plenty of family and guests. She was wired ten thousand dollars for her valuable information.

When Paco received the information from his cousin, he valued that for what it was worth because his cousin was not a bullshit artist. Plus, she knew how fucking crazy her little cousin was. He would kill one of his own family members for the right price. He didn't tell Baby Hatchet right away. He held on to the info until his boss was sweating bullets out of fear for his life, then he unleashed in on Baby Hatchet one day while they were arguing on the phone about The Terribles not producing results.

"You say that my crew are not on their job. Well I say that you are wrong, because I have people up in Newark and Irvington, New Jersey that are scouting all of the hair salons and clubs and they have recently came through with very resourceful information about Pretty Boy's sister and his enforcer Diablo who are getting married soon and vacationing down here in South Beach for their honeymoon. Can you fucking believe that shit boss?" exclaimed Paco into the telephone.

"Are you fucking kidding me or what? Are you serious? Have you known about this long Paco?" asked Baby Hatchet. "When are they supposed to be getting married, where is the wedding going to be, and where in South Beach are they going to be staying?" he continued to ask Paco.

"Whoa, whoa, slow down a little bit boss. We have what we have to work with and we have to make the best of the information we have because we cannot afford to fuck this up. All she gave me was the month of the wedding and the month of the honeymoon. They are getting married in September, so I would count on the honeymoon being in October," Paco said to Baby Hatchet.

"Then October is the month for retribution!" remarked a recuperating Baby Hatchet.

Baby Hatchet couldn't wait to tell all of Ms. Cuba's brothers that he had a serious lead on the 50/50 Crew, and a sure way to penetrate their defenses by kidnapping Pretty Boy's sister after they tortured and killed her new husband during their honeymoon in a few months. Baby Hatchet's cocaine connection seemed to be pleased with what they were promised. Still, they were eager to show Baby Hatchet that they were not playing around, so to give Baby Hatchet some inspiration, they had little Troublesome and little Viper from The Terribles murdered at a Taco Bell on the Eastside.

As The Terribles and Baby Hatchet were getting closer and closer to getting to the 50/50 Crew, Gorilla was slowly but surely getting closer to Baby Hatchet.

Chapter 7
Time to Go To War

Meanwhile, up in Newark, New Jersey, the remaining members of the 50/50 Crew that stayed behind were about to get into a serious beef that was thought to be squashed but was only put off to the side to be later dealt with by the Nigerians that Uzi Malik had violated before he fled to Florida.

The Nigerians had been successfully dealing heroin in Newark for almost fifteen years now without any problems, until they encountered the 50/50 Crew. They had food businesses (wholesale butcher shops and restaurants), churches, and car dealerships all from the heroin trade in Essex County, and they were not about to let anyone take their respect or shame them in the streets of any state!

They were all millionaires as well, and they knew the risks involved if they engaged in a major beef with the 50/50 Crew but they didn't give a fuck. All they cared about was money, power, and respect. They had not forgotten about the loss they took when Uzi Malik that was affiliated with the 50/50 Crew killed some of their main people and caused a tremendous decrease in their normal profits. In retaliation to the attempted murder of Uzi Malik, the 50/50 Crew leaders decided to send a response in the form of two bombings of the Nigerians' car lots and two murders of a captain and a lieutenant within the organization of the Nigerians. They were now bent on revenge and as the world knows, it is a dish best served cold.

With Speechless, Gorilla, and Chinky in Florida handling other important business, Pretty Boy and Shorty Slice were left to run things up in New Jersey which was never a problem for them at all. The problem was the sudden events occurring at the blocks and territories that the 50/50 Crew ruled. There were several robberies, aggravated assaults, and even a few murders of soldiers employed by the 50/50 Crew. Blocks that normally produced fifty-thousand dollars a week were now only bringing in twenty-thousand dollars in profits weekly, and Shorty Slice and Pretty Boy were determined to figure this problem out and solve it before their brothers got back from Miami with Baby Hatchet's head, and a healthy Chinky.

"There is too much fucking money not being made due to these setbacks with the workers Pretty Boy and I am telling you bro, that this shit has the fucking Africans written all over it," Shorty Slice said to Pretty Boy.

"True that. It seems like they waited to see if our brothers were going to surface anytime soon, and when they realized that they were out of town, or word hit the streets that they were, all of a sudden they want to fucking flex and continue this beef over the motherfuckers that U.M. had murdered when Shotgun Shawn was killed. That shit is old news, but it is going to bring some new drama for sure. Get the teams together and tell them to grip the fuck up, we are going to give these fucking Nigerians a nice surprise and a reminder not to fuck with the 50/50 Crew!" barked Pretty Boy.

"Roger that bro, I am on that immediately!" replied Shorty Slice.

The very next morning after their discussion, the 50/50 Crew hit the Nigerians early around seven a.m., when their dope blocks were at their apex. Equipped with four stolen cars loaded with four armed shooters each car, the sixteen locked and loaded gangsters headed towards the areas where the Nigerians pumped heroin from five in the morning until eight p.m. everyday including Sundays. They were gripped with everything from Uzis to Intratech-9s, and 380s to Desert Eagles of various calibers and they were some of the most accurate gunners on the 50/50 Crew's payroll. The plan was simple; One car ride through each block with everyone shooting except the driver and when they got to the end of the block, send another car up the opposite side of the street to make sure whoever didn't get shot, got shot! They repeated this four more times that particular morning in four different areas, and the results were devastating to the Nigerians organization, costing them millions of dollars after their streets were shut down for the next six months with the police installing mini sub-stations on every corner of the massacres. An unbelievable total of seventy people were murdered and another twenty injured when the 50/50 Crew hit up the Nigerians on that bloody morning, and thirty of the dead were dope fiends.

Olutu "The Leopard" Olujabu, the chief boss of the Nigerians crew was beyond infuriated; he was vexed and full of retribution. He told his top captains Devil and Demon to make some waves because of this violation. "Some bloody fucking tidal waves!" he ordered.

All of the top hierarchy in the Nigerians organization went by African animal nicknames: The Leopard, The Lion, Cheetah, Hyena, and Tiger. They were all also blood related and very close, since surviving the turmoil of West Africa and fleeing to the United States. There was no hate or envy amongst them, because they all were very, very rich.

Meanwhile, Pretty Boy and Shorty Slice were relishing in their victory and the success of their hits on the Nigerians. They were out having fun with the ladies, partying and enjoying life. They popped bottles and smoked the best up in the V.I.P. section of the biggest club in Newark, with the most beautiful ladies accompanying them, as well as ten gunmen. They knew that shit was going to get thick real soon, but they were the same old gangsters that didn't give a fuck back when they were locked up at heart; tough as fucking nails! They spent about ten thousand on bottles and food fucking around with their 50/50 Crew enforcers and a few model-status females from out Plainfield and Union. Motherfuckers even danced a little, happy that their brother Chinky was safe and healthy and with the goons strapped up watching their backs, they partied care-fucking-free. After the club, they checked into their individual suites at the Marquis overlooking the water and enjoyed life for the night.

Pretty Boy was always up early as shit, and so was Shorty Slice. It was an automatic thing that happens after you are away for a while doing time. Gradually your body adjusts to the normal times of waking up but it takes time. They were both up at around five a.m. and were checking out at seven. They would allow the ladies to stay as long as they wanted to before check-out time. They hit they highway and got back to the hood quick. Then ate breakfast in Irvington before splitting in different directions to go get right for the day.

Two weeks after the hits on the Nigerians, the production of the drug strips the 50/50 Crew ran were beginning to pick up and show signs of progress. The blocks that normally did fifty thousand dollars a week were now pushing out thirty-five and forty geez each week, and things were getting back on track. Pretty Boy was preparing for his sisters' wedding that was coming up really soon, and she was marrying his personal enforcer, so he couldn't have been more proud.

He offered to pay for the wedding, something that his father would have done had he still been around, and he was flying everyone to Puerto Rico for the wedding ceremony. His younger sister Melissa loved visiting the state of Florida so much, that she convinced her husband-to-be, Diablo, to have her honeymoon in South Beach Miami. All in all, Pretty Boy was spending about six-hundred thousand dollars on the gifts and wedding for his sister and best homeboy.

Diablo had been loyal to Pretty Boy ever since Chinky replaced him with Dolly after Dolly had become Chinky's personal bodyguard/enforcer. There was no love lost between Chinky and Diablo because they still remained family, it was a tight circle anyway. He and Shorty Slice made sure that the money was all accounted for and that the books were straight for the 50/50 Crew as a collective, and to make sure shit was right, they sent goons into territories that they didn't give a fuck about to kick in a couple of doors and get that money up!

They would never look as though they couldn't handle business on their own in the eyes of their brothers, or anyone else for that matter. They knew what they had to do and they got it done. They were bosses. More than anything though, it was pride that kept them for paying and making up for loses out of their own money (although they all were millionaires). If they took a loss behind the actions of someone else, then they simply took it out on someone else's bankroll!

Pretty Boy wanted to make sure that everything was going to be perfect for his little sisters' wedding, so he went all out and brought them a Mercedes limo as a wedding gift as well, though the lucky couple would not find that out until the very end of the wedding when they were preparing to drive off. He had already made travel arrangements for the entire wedding party, including the limo surprise and Diablo didn't need to spend a dime. All he had to do was stay true to Melissa and protect her and their family always.

Together she and Diablo owned several small businesses: two nail salons, a grocery store, and a small ninety-five-person total capacity restaurant that catered to Spanish-Americans. They would make a great life together for themselves and a very prosperous living for their two children little Danny and Delilah.

Melissa Maria Gonzalez was four years younger than her older brother Ricky, and she was always sheltered and protected as a young girl growing up in the rough section of North Newark. She was very, very beautiful and had flowing long hair, and even as early as thirteen years old she was very curvy, thanks to her Puerto Rican mother. They kept her in Catholic school all the way from elementary through high school, and when it was time for her to go to college, she had met Diablo through her brother, and fell in love with him. She got pregnant and they moved in together immediately. Then two years later she was pregnant with their daughter and they moved into a house in Bloomfield very close to North Newark. There was never any infidelity in their relationship because she loved him hard and unconditionally and he was employed by her brother, it was that simple. Diablo knew better. They had no domestic issues either for the same reasons. They were busy everyday planning and rearranging details of their dream wedding on the beach, and in Puerto Rico where their mothers was born. Diablo was also half Dominican on his fathers' side. They spent days adding or cancelling invitations. She knew that no matter how many family and friends she invited that her big brother would pay for it regardless.

Diablo, also known by his born name, Ramon Dominguez, was loyal to his North Newark roots and loyal to Pretty Boy's family. He grew up rough and became rough quick in the barrio of their area, advancing swiftly to the ranks of enforcer and personal bodyguard because of his taste for violence. He was well-known in his hood and well-respected everywhere in North Newark, but he only ate in his section. When he began to work for Pretty Boy, his brother-in-law-to-be had rapidly excelled and was making tons of money with his 50/50 Crew partners in the dope game.

Pretty boy and Chinky had clearly inherited their hustling abilities and survival skills from their fathers no doubt. They were both in the feds now doing life for CCE and they weren't ever going to be free men again, but they still ran shit in their individual prisons on the dope tip. Diablo had lost both of his parents to crack and heroin addictions when he was young, so he was raised by his mothers' sister, his auntie Nancy. When he started making lots of money working for Pretty Boy, he made sure he had took care of his aunt that had taken such good care of him for many years by buying her a house and a brand-new car. Now here he was, getting ready to marry the woman of his dreams and into a family that was very well-respected abroad in just a few months. "How time flies," he thought to himself constantly.

Shorty Slice and Pretty Boy were out making rounds in separate parts of town. Pretty Boy was running around Ivy Hill, Hillside, and Irvington and Shorty Slice was dipping in and out of Weequahic, Down the Hill, and the Westside section of Newark, collecting money for the team. The other spots that they had weren't ready with their weekly drop-offs yet, and they would see them another time during the week to collect. When Shorty Slice pulled up to a red light at the corner of 16th Ave and 15th Street near West Side Park, two motorcycles driven by Africans no doubt, cut him off and started blasting right there in the middle of the street at his car. Of course, the vehicle he was in was bullet-proof everywhere.

All of the 50/50 Crew rolled like that since the wars started way back when. He immediately mashed on the gas and ran one of them the fuck over with the entire left side of his Audi truck, crushing him almost completely as the other assassin fled through the park. Shorty Slice hit Pretty Boy on the phone and quickly told him what was going down and where he was as he chased the motorcycle. He drove straight down 18th Avenue and made a left at the bottom of the hill where the park ends so that he could cut off the bike on 19th Avenue when he came out on the other side.

He could see the motorcycle-driven shooter fleeing through the park clearly through the railed gate that surrounded West Side Park, and he was very close to the bike now. He reached on the passenger seat and picked the gun he had taken out of the glove box when they first started shooting. Then, rolling down the window, slowly taking aim slightly ahead of the motorcycle then he let off four of the six shots that the .38 revolver held. One of the bullets struck the driver in the shoulder and another hit the front tire somewhere because the bike flipped forward throwing the driver about eight feet into the street of 19th Avenue.

Shorty Slice quickly pulled over and got out running towards the biker. He had the .38 in his right hand as he got close up on the twisted body of the shooter and shot him twice in the face.

Pretty Boy was going coming down 17th Avenue and 18th Street when his phone rang, it was Shorty Slice.

"Meet me at WC ASAP bro! History books!" Shorty Slice told Pretty Boy. WC was code for White Castles in Irvington. History books meant that he took care of the threat.

"Okay bro, see you soon," replied Pretty Boy.

While sitting in the parking lot of White Castle, they discussed further action against the aggressive Nigerians. It was time to strike at the head and cause some serious damage to these violators.

"Listen bro, we can get at these motherfuckers through these bitches man, these chumps have a serious weakness for pussy Pretty Boy I'm telling you!" exclaimed Shorty Slice.

"Really? Do they now? Then let's set this shit in motion bro. Find out where their bitches, wives, and baby mamas get their hair and nails done! Send the shooters right up in that motherfucker up close and personal, fuck that. Hit these bitches where they will hurt the most!" barked Pretty Boy, getting angrier with every word he spoke.

Two weeks later, on Monday, Thursday, and Saturday of the same week, three of the heads of the Nigerian mob lost their significant other to war violence. Lion lost his wife Jaguar, as she was violently gunned down in a robbery attempt of a beauty salon she owned in Maplewood. Cheetah's mistress and her best friend were both shot in the head as they sat in the parking lot waiting for the crowd to settle down in the nail salon they had made appointments in so that they could go inside. And The Leopard lost his twins' mother when a firebomb blew up the hair and nail boutique she had owned for ten years out in Short Hills, killing her and six others inside. His four-year-old twin sons, nicknamed Panther and Jag because they were as dark-complexioned as their father, were out at Chucky Cheese with the kids of his brothers and cousins, celebrating one of the little ones' birthday, so they were lucky not to be with their mother on that day.

In retaliation, the Nigerians would be merciless and emotionless with their revenge on the 50/50 Crew. The Leopard, Cheetah, Hyena, Lion and Tiger all met up at their lodge up in Livingston for a sit down to discuss the demise of the 50/50 Crew.

"I am telling you bruddas, that these muddafuckas are fucking ruthless man. They kill our women without evening blinking a fucking eye. These bastards are dead men fucking walking!" barked The Leopard.

"I agree brudda. Total fucking disregard for human life with these guys. Time to put an end to all of dis dumb shit now!" replied Hyena.

"Yes!" screamed out Tiger. "All of these muddafuckas must die! Fuck da dumb shit!" Tiger continued to rant.

"They treat us like we are fucking nobodies in dis game. Now these pussy muddafuckas will feel our wrath and know that the Nigerians are nothing to be toyed with, in any way!" remarked Cheetah.

"Cheetah, you still in contact with them white bitches from Canada right? What do dey call themselves? The Chinchillas, right?" asked The Leopard.

"Yes, that be them Leopard, The Chinchillas. White girls with just a touch of black on them or in them. Ha, ha, ha, ha, ha! Those bitches are some down ass bitches and they will do anything for dat almighty dollar bruddas!" said Cheetah.

"Call them now!" Leopard commanded.

Rose, Blossom, Tulips, Ivy, Daisy, and Dandi were all members of a killer elite crew of dime piece white girls from Ontario, Canada that called themselves The Chinchillas. They all had big juicy asses that rivaled any video vixen of any nationality, long hair, and the coolest attitudes any man would love to encounter, but they were deadly and delicious at the same time. For years, they had taken contracts from mob bosses, drug dealers, and even police that wanted fellow officers wacked because they were either a rat or getting ready to turn. They were white girls that talked, walked, and acted as cool as any Black or Latino girl did, and they were always welcome to all of the parties and get-togethers throughout numerous cities, both in Canada and the U.S.

They killed for a living sure, but that was their side-hustle. Their main source of income was growing a selling large amounts of the loudest marijuana around. They grossed hundreds of thousands of dollars each year from their marijuana business and no one dared to fuck with them after years of making examples out of dumb motherfuckers. Their weakness, like any other white chick, was black dick! These bitches would kill and have killed over their men. They all had men that were black, or if they weren't involved, they just strictly dealt with black men only and the darker the better for them.

Rose, the main leader of The Chinchillas, had sold some pounds to Cheetah of the Nigerians mob years ago and started to have a relationship with him immediately. She was very attracted to his swagger, money, and the way he put it down in bed. He and his African mob had a lot of money and they wore a lot of gold and silk. They looked like kings of the hood to Rose when she had met them all. Ten months after dealing with Rose, Cheetah had her traveling to Newark, New Jersey on a regular basis just to get fucked royally and then, one day he found out about her other talents.

"What is stressing you out so much?" she asked him one day years ago after they had just finished fucking and she noticed his demeanor.

"Nothing woman. Not your business, nothing you can do!" he snapped at her.

"Are you sure about that? You haven't even told me what the issue is yet, so how can you say I can do nothing to assist you baby?" she reminded him.

"There are some muddafuckas standing in our way where we are trying to make money and after we sent them a message, they shot up my cousin and killed him in response. So can you help me with that Ms. Snow White?" he asked her sarcastically.

"Absolutely. For the right price me and my girls wills wipe out the whole lot of them motherfuckers that are causing you problems. How many people are we talking about erasing?" Rose asked Cheetah. He just looked at her shocked.

"Are you serious? This is no muddafucking joke girl, do not play games!" he stated.

"We don't play any motherfucking games playboy. We are about that business straight up, and for twenty-five thousand dollars a head, I can show you that we are about that business Cheetah," she said to him.

One month after that first conversation about his problems and one-hundred thousand dollars later, The Chinchillas had taken out Rafael Guzman and his three brothers Raul, Pablo, and Miguel Guzman who had the entire Ironbound section in Newark on lockdown with the raw heroin. After that, the Nigerians had exploded and expanded across the map of Newark like wildfire and Cheetah would use The Chinchillas two more times to help the Nigerians; once in Jersey City and again in Elizabeth.

Cheetah placed a call to Rose.

"Hello, what's good Cheetah baby? Do you miss this bomb-ass head and tail or what?" Rose flirted. She loved to swallow and get fucked in the ass.

"Of course, of course I do, and I need to see you and your team as soon as possible woman, can you get here tomorrow?" he asked Rose.

"Sure thing my dark prince and I will bring some of that good shit you like to choke on too," she replied.

When The Chinchillas arrived at Newark International Airport, they were greeted by a Mercedes S600 stretch limo that was flanked by two Mercedes GL 500 trucks. They felt like diplomats riding in style all the way from Newark to Livingston, where the Nigerians had two different headquarters located. Taking in the scenery, as the road the s-turns passing South Mountain Reservation in South Orange on their way to Livingston, the ladies anticipated their meeting with the Nigerian heads.

As they pulled in to the massive parking lot of a church, the gates came up at the checkpoint and they were allowed entry.

As they stop and the doors were opened for them, they were greeted by two heavily armed guards that didn't smile or say a word. They just stood there holding AR-15 automatic rifles. When the enormous doors of the church opened up, The Chinchillas could see that there were pews everywhere and there were also plenty of chairs and tables; the place was huge! They were escorted past all of the scenery they had taken in, and brought down a long corridor that led to a big office. Inside of the office, all of the heads of the Nigerian mob sat in a chair draped with his namesakes' skin, except for The Lion, whom had a lions' head also atop his chair, giving it the appearance of a throne.

"Welcome ladies! Please have a seat and get as comfortable as you possibly can. I am The Leopard, and these are my bruddas Hyena, Tiger, Lion, and you already know Cheetah," The Lion said.

"Nice to meet you Mr. Leopard. I am Rose, and these are my Chinchillas Blossom, Tulips, Ivy, Dandi, and Daisy. We are at your service. What can we do for you all?" Rose said, maintaining eye-contact with The Leopard as she spoke.

"What we have is a fucking problem and what we need is this fucking problem solved immediately!" Yelled The Leopard.

"Who are they? When are we getting paid, and where do you want their heads delivered to? How much is a job like this going to pay my team?" she asked.

"I like her. She has courage, I can tell," Tiger spoke up.

"The job is a five-man crew of muddafukas that no longer need to be on dis earth. Right now, the focus is only two of dem," he said, as he tossed the envelope across the table to her. "Their names are Shorty Slice and the Spanish-looking one, his name is Pretty Boy. They are two of the five bosses in this crew. The job pays two-hundred and fifty thousand dollars a head!" He concluded.

"Is that right?" asked Blossom as she took the envelope Rose handed her and examined the photographs of their targets. "Two-hundred and fifty geez per fucking head. Sweet. When do we start?" she asked again.

"You start now," said Hyena, tossing Ivy a bag of money with one-hundred thousand dollars inside of it. "Here's fifty-thousand per head up front. If the job is not complete within the next two weeks, we will take this as a sign of failure and two of your team will be murdered to compensate for our loss, agreed?" Hyena continued.

Rose hesitated at the sound of her girls lives' being threatened right in front of her. Then, she looked around at all of her team and said,

"We are in!"

After the adjourning of their meeting, they ate spicy African dishes that were prepared by private African chefs, smoked ounces of good weed and drank plenty of liquor before splitting up into pairs and fucking all night long. There was long week ahead for The Chinchillas, but they just couldn't resist the dark-skinned bosses that seemed to be so attracted to them.

Chapter 8
Pretty Boy

Ever since Pretty Boy was young, watching his father and uncles hustle in the streets getting money and respect everywhere, he knew that he was going to be a hustler. It wasn't until he and Chinky's fathers were imprisoned while he was locked up, that he had decided to be a "full-time" hustler. After his father had ordered the murder of the father of the two brothers that jumped his son in school, the investigation increased and the family got hot. They came in full-force with all of the federal charges they could muster and half of them stuck, condemning them to life in prison and their co-defendants the same. No one snitched in their organization and the rest of the team that were free and didn't get wrapped-up took care of the families of those incarcerated. Once young Pretty Boy went to jail and met young Speechless and young Shorty Slice, he was really ready for the game because he heard that his childhood best friend/brother was now in the game holding down the crew. There was no question about it; he was in it until death do us.

When they completed their crew with young Gorilla, there was no stopping the new 50/50 Crew. They went where they wanted and got money, setting up shop wherever the fuck they wanted to in the process of progress. They were relentless in their grind, their wrath, and their focus. By the time they were in their twenties, Pretty Boy was a millionaire and so was every other founding member/boss of the 50/50 Crew. They had in all and then some and nothing stopped them from getting more.

As he sat in his teal-green Mercedes coupe at the right light on Springfield Avenue and Grove Street waiting to drive up and go check out some new turf up in Vaux Hall, he thought about his brothers down in Miami and wondered when the hell they would be done down there so that they could collectively deal with the Nigerians, and put a definite end to this beef. He headed up Springfield Ave. when the light turned green and made all the other green lights until he hit Irvington Center, near the bus terminal. That's when he dialed Speechless to check on things down in Florida.

"Hello, Pretty Boy what's good brother, and how are things going with you two up the way?" asked Speechless when he answered his cell on the first ring seeing it was Pretty Boy.

"You already know shit is good on this end we are handing business as usual and all of the companies (dope spots they ran together) are doing well, and profits are the same. Shorty Slice is Shorty Slice, regular shit with him. Nothing changed here, but we want to know what's good down there and when is the vacation going to be over?" stated Pretty Boy.

"Soon, trying to close up this deal now and just got some great information on the location of some prime real estate, location of their intended target, Baby Hatchet, so I am going to send Gorilla meet with the guy and close that deal," replied Speechless.

"That's great news. We miss our brothers and we wanted to make sure things were going smoothly with the investments down there, send crew love to Chinky and Gorilla for me and be safe down there my brother. One!" concluded Pretty Boy. He never once mentioned the ongoing mini-war with the vindictive Africans to Speechless.

"Sure will, tell Shorty Slice the same. One!" Said Speechless, hanging up his cell and continuing his drive to meet with a new reliable source that supposedly knew exactly where Baby Hatchet was hiding out.

When Pretty Boy hit the upper Irvington are and crossed into Maplewood, he knew that he had to be easy with his music and driving because the police in those rural suburban areas didn't play but they did profile a motherfucker for sure. He got to Vaux Hall without incident and met with his peoples Apache up there, that was from Clinton Avenue and Grace Street in Irvington, and nothing had changed with Apache from the time they were walking the yard together on the inside. He was still a down ass crazy motherfucker.

"What's the deal playboy? It's good to see you A, how the hell have you been my brother?" asked Pretty Boy, as he climbed out of the Benz coupe and greeted Apache, who was one of the two kids walking with young Pretty Boy when he had initially met with young Speechless and young Shorty Slice in the Bordentown jail.

"How are you is the question? You the playboy nigga, look at the spaceship you are getting out of Pretty Boy. Heard a lot of big things about you man," replied Apache. Apache was Dominican, a natural born soldier and he loved to get that paper. He was the same age as Pretty Boy, but he was taller and bigger at six foot one and two hundred and forty pounds. He wore his hair in long braids, and he got it redone every week so his hairstyle was always fresh, which the girls always admired. He was up in Vaux Hall for two years now after getting into a beef in Irvington that ended in someone being shot, and he needed more of that white product to take over more territory. Vaux Hall was very small, and was about thirty-five percent Black, fifteen percent Latino, and fifty percent Caucasian. Apache had about fifteen percent of that fifty percent in his phone, as people who bought coke from him. He also sold weed as well, and his customer-base was much larger for that specific item, but he brought that from someone else who had a serious Canadian connection for the good green at very low rates.

"Everything is good with me bro, and I am here to make sure that everything is good with you also. Time to expand and take you up on your invitation to capitalize on this area up here. You still the main dude up here correct?" asked Pretty Boy.

"Of course I am bro, nobody is doing shit up here but me and two other cats and they are buying from me!" replied Apache. "Motherfuckers know better than to try and open up shop without my acknowledgement or involvement. I will swiss cheese this whole fucking town and head elsewhere before I let somebody takes chunks out of what I pioneered up here, fuck that!" he continued to say.

"Same old Apache, I hear you. That's what the fuck I need to hear because if you are good with the 50/50 crew, then the 50/50 Crew is good with you understand?" Pretty Boy stated.

"Yes I do, clearly," Apache replied.

They ironed out the details of their arrangement after Apache took Pretty Boy on a brief tour of the territory and showed him the visual of that geographical area. Pretty Boy had to admit to himself that the new turf would most definitely bring in lots of money and quietly too. Immediately he would be given ten kilos of the best cocaine in Essex

County, and soon he would have a little piece of Union County as well. They had six pairs of eyes on them the whole time.

After seeing Apache straight and making the necessary pick-ups for that part of the day, Pretty Boy called his shorty up on the phone for a quickie.

"Hello, where are you at?" Miranda asked right off the bat.

"On my way to see you gorgeous, are you ready for me?" He asked one of his main side-pieces.

"Hell yes, you know I am always ready for you daddy. Hurry the fuck up and get here!" she demanded.

"Okay, be there in fifteen minutes," he said, hanging up the phone and dialing Shorty Slice.

"Brother what's up? Where are you at?" asked Shorty Slice when he answered on the first ring.

"On my way out to Linden to go fuck the shit out of Miranda real quick and get back to the town. What's good with you bro? Everything good so far as far as the Africans go?" Pretty Boy inquired.

"You just can't get enough of that little hot Dominican treasure pot huh brother? Didn't she get married last year?" asked Shorty Slice. "Everything is good on my end though. I got a few shooters flanking me in the Range Rover, you already know. They won't let a car get between us!" he continued.

"Okay then, I will touch base with you when I get back. Hit me if any emergencies and be safe," Pretty boy concluded.

"Right, be safe," Shorty Slice replied.

Pretty Boy stepped on the accelerator and pushed the Benz coupe on the freeway through Elizabeth and got off near Linden and Carteret.

Miranda Matos was one hundred percent Dominican, and as gorgeous as a beauty pageant winner. She was twenty-four years old and would have probably been Pretty Boy's wife if she didn't strip for a living and travel so much while she did it. She was five feet four inches tall barefoot, and her hair came down to the top of her ass. She had gorgeous hazel eyes and pretty teeth, and her main feature was her body. She had a body that belonged in magazine and video shoots. Hourglass-figure was an understatement! She fell in love with Pretty Boy three years ago when they met at a strip club in Elizabeth where she danced at the time. He was out there making moves for the 50/50 Crew with a couple of big-time dealers from out that way, when she approached him with an unopened bottle of water and asked if he was thirsty. When he turned towards her to give her his undivided attention, she caught him off guard with all of her stunning beauty and features.

"Hell yeah I am thirsty beautiful, thirsty for you. What's good with you baby doll and what time do you get off tonight? What's your name gorgeous? I'm Pretty Boy, it's nice to make your acquaintance," Pretty Boy asked her, flashing his perfect smile and displaying his diamond & platinum jewelry in her face as he took her.

"Miranda is my name, but when I am working, it's Paradise because that's where they are when they fantasize about being with me," she said, displaying a dazzling smile of her own.

"Is that right Ma? So are you leaving when I leave here or what Ms. Miranda?" Pretty Boy pressed her.

"If you are staying until two a.m., then I guess I am leaving with you handsome," she replied, once again flashing that beautiful smile at him, then walking away looking back seductively at him over her shoulder from time to time as she faded into the crowd, switching her perfect ass back and forth.

It was only 12:52 a.m. when they met at the bar that night, but he would stay until her shift ended.

After taking care of business with the people he came to see, he left the club with Miranda and went straight to the Diner in Irvington because the local diners always ended up in drama and gunshots when the hustlers from Newark would drift into Union County. When he got to Don's, it was packed as usual but he had pull with the manager and was seated immediately as if he had reservations. She was impressed instantly. He ordered steak and eggs for the both of them and an extra plate of cheese eggs on the side that they would share. He also ordered orange juices and dry wheat toast for them as well. Over breakfast, they got familiar and talked about everything from her aspirations to his dreams of owning twenty businesses in the state New Jersey alone. They laughed and joked like they had known each other for at least a month, though it was only hours ago they had met.

"Do you work tonight?" he asked her.

"I am supposed to. Why? What did you have in mind Pretty Boy?" she asked him, showing a little devious smile.

"Kissing all over your pretty shoulders after I wash your beautiful hair in the shower," he stated.

"Let's get out of here," Miranda said.

That early morning, he had taken her out to the airport to a top-rate hotel and they stayed the entire day until they had breakfast the very next morning. During the evening they had room service. They spent time together three times a week since that first night they had met, for the last two years. And then she met her husband, some bozo that played professional baseball for a New York team. She had gotten married a year ago, but every time that her husband was on the road playing or out in Las Vegas gambling, she would call Pretty Boy up to play with her. He just happened to be thinking about her while he was up in Vaux Hall with Apache because he was in Union County and she was clearly the finest bitch he ever fucked with from Union County.

When he pulled up at her apartment that she kept on the side in Linden, she and her professional husband had a humungous house out in Woodbridge together, she was standing in the doorway because she knew from the time she had spoken with him that he wouldn't be long getting there. He never kept her waiting as long as she had known him. She was as sexy as ever, standing there with nothing on but a short tee-shirt and some spandex work-out shorts, barefoot.

He climbed out of the coupe and walked up the steps to her awaiting arms, hugged her, then kissed her on the forehead and walked into the apartment. As soon as they were in the foyer, she stripped off his pants and boxer briefs and started sucking him off hungrily. She had missed him dearly since her marriage and she wanted to show him just how much. Once she sucked him to orgasm, she got up and led him to her bedroom, all the while looking back at him looking at her fat juicy ass as she seductively sashayed her hips back and forth. When they got to the bedroom, he locked the door, out of habit, and took the rest of his clothes and jewelry off, then he started to tear her ass up after he put the Magnum on.

He fucked her every way there was to be fucked within an hour, then they showered and she gave him the ass in the shower. After she had used the enema, there was no need for any lube because she naturally got gushy for him and he just used the juices from her own pussy to lubricate her asshole as he fucked her hard in her ass; something that she absolutely loved and her lame ass husband refused to do. She climaxed over and over again, and then he came in in her ass; something that he could never resist. She would sometimes ask him,

"Why do you use a condom when you fuck me in my pussy but when I want anal, you just use your dick Pretty Boy?" she asked him, and his reply would always be the same.

"I trust you baby, and I know that you stay on top of your duties keeping that treasure chest perfect but you can't get pregnant from me nutting in your ass Ma. We will never make any mistakes as long as we keep it like this. Besides, I love busting in your fat ass baby," he would tell her. She loved to hear that shit.

After they had finished fucking and showering, they smoked some good-good, she sucked him off again, and then he breezed back to Newark to finish handling business. He had been out there with Miranda for damn near three hours.

When he got back to his area, he reached out to his sister to see if she was ready for the big plunge next month, and he teased her about seeing Diablo's face for the rest of her life.

"You sure you are ready to do this baby sister?" he asked her over the phone.

"Yes silly, of course I am sure big brother, and it couldn't be to a better man. I mean, you trusted him with your life for all these years so that I know that you are going to trust him with mine, and your niece and nephews'," she stated.

"Just checking, just checking Melissa. Sometimes women get cold feet you know. The men do too and at the last minute these things don't go through. I just want to make sure that my baby sister doesn't get hurt in any way, but I know Diablo got you, so no worries over here. How are the kids?" Pretty Boy asked.

"They are fine, and we are good boy stop worrying ok," she said.

"Yeah, I will stop worrying when this is over and you two are married already!" he said.

"Okay, and how are you doing Mr. Pretty Ricky?" she asked jokingly.

"I am good sis, real good. I will see you soon," he concluded, ending the call. He never noticed the white Altima that had followed him from Vaux Hall to Linden, and now that it was nightfall, they were following him to Shorty Slice.

When he pulled up at one of their businesses, the rib & wing joint they all owned together, it was thriving with business and the parking lot was just as crowded. He went inside and straight to the back, down a long corridor of the old laundromat converted into a fast-food spot, and entered one of the offices. Shorty Slice was in their counting up money and banding it up in ten-thousand-dollar stacks when Pretty boy came in, and he asked him to join in on the money counting.

"Don't just stand there and watch me bro, grab yourself some money and get to counting would you please?" Shorty Slice asked mockingly.

"Will do. Now pass me one of them money bags will you," Pretty Boy said as he grabbed the pre-counted money out of the bags they had picked up from their numerous drug spots around town.

They had counted and re-counted nine hundred eighty-one thousand dollars and then they bagged it up in two duffels and prepared to move it to one of the main stashes of the 50/50 crew. Carrying a duffel bag each, they left the office and walked down the corridor with two shooters in front of them and one behind them, flanking them. When they approached the main part of the restaurant where the patrons waited to order or receive their food, they noticed some out-of-place white chicks that were fine as hell, but looked as if they were passing through the hood looking for some drug dealers they probably had met at Atlantic City or down the shore somewhere. Two of them were at the counter and two of them were near the exits. Then the gunshots went off. POP, POP, POP! POP, POP, POP! BOOM! BOOM! BBRRRAT!, BBRRAT! BRAT! TAT! TAT! POP, POP, POP! People ran everywhere in any direction they could, even running into each other in a frantic panic as four of The Chinchillas stood with their backs up against the wall and the counter and just dumped bullet after bullet in the direction of Pretty Boy, Shorty Slice, and their shooters, with heavy artillery that was provided by the Nigerians. They shot many innocent people, but they didn't care because to them, the bystanders were just shields in the way of their targets.

The first two 50/50 Crew shooters, Bags and Snake that were in front of them caught it bad, shot in the face and chest with shotgun blasts, as Pretty Boy and Shorty Slice ducked down just in time to avoid the powerful impact of the shotgun and machine gun the assassins were obviously using. Pulling their own weapons when they realized that it was a hit and not a robbery, the two 50/50 Crew leaders squeezed off shots from their 17-shot Berettas in the direction of the female shooters, dropping the one that had the shotgun, and another one wielding a 9mm, as they fled the side entrance of the rib & wing joint. Pretty Boy was struck in the rear left shoulder and left elbow as they ran from the fast food spot frantically scrambling to get to one of their vehicles. If they could just make it to the car.

"I'm hit Shorty! They got me bro! I'm hit and I can't feel my left arm!" yelled Pretty Boy, as he and their last shooter ran behind Shorty Slice and towards the truck Shorty Slice was driving.

"Hold on Pretty Boy, we got you brother!" Shorty Slice yelled back to him, as he stopped and let off a fresh clip at the female assassins, striking another one of them in the face and throat. Police sirens could be heard approaching a few blocks away.

"I'm empty!" Pretty Boy said to Shorty Slice.

"Here take this, and get to the stash house. Call the Doc and have him meet you there, go!" he yelled to Pretty Boy, passing him the duffle bag and his keys to the whip. "These bitches done fucked with the wrong fucking crew. This shit has Africans written all over it!" he continued to yell, as he fired shot after shot. "Go now!" he yelled again at Pretty Boy, as they ducked down in between some parked cars.

Pretty Boy grabbed the keys and other duffle bag from Shorty Slice, gave him a look, and ran across the street to Shorty Slice's Audi Q5. He managed to get in and get it started, then speed off down the block as he could see Shorty Slice and one of their shooters, D-Money, holding court with the bitches.

As he stopped at the corner, Pretty Boy couldn't help to think that Shorty Slice might not have enough extra clips on him to survive the shoot-out. So even though he was bleeding excessively and wounded badly, with his left arm damn near numb, he had to check on his brother. He made two right turns, and was right back where the rib & wing joint was just in time to see some white bitch in a white jumpsuit and black boots hop out of a white Nissan Altima shooting D-Money down. D-Money didn't even see the bitch coming at him and caught two to the head and one in the spine area.

He was dead when he hit the ground. Pretty Boy mashed on the gas as he saw the same bitch trying to line-up Shorty Slice in her sights, and plowed right into her, smashing her up against a blue Chevy van next to her Altima, killing her instantly. As he pulled the Audi Q5 back away from the wreckage, he opened the glove box and grabbed a loaded 40. Caliber, then he blew the horn at Shorty Slice and signaled for him to meet him in the middle of the street so that he could pick him up. Shorty Slice started running towards the Audi truck, shooting at the women killers as it seemed to be more of them emerging from nowhere, but it was the same hit squad.

The bitches had bullet-proof vests on that were also provided by the Nigerians. He got hit in the back of the right leg as he was almost to the truck, then a high-caliber bullet struck him in the back of the head blowing away his nose and the upper part of his mouth, and he fell dead at the foot of the passenger–side of his own truck, just inches away from the door handle. Pretty Boy was stunned. The sirens got louder.

"Shorty Slice!" yelled Pretty Boy, as he rolled the window all the way down and shot at the bitch that held the machine gun that had just killed Shorty Slice. "Shorty Slice! OH SHIT!" BANG! BANG! "Motherfuckers." BANG! BANG! "Killed." BANG! BANG! BANG! "My." BANG! BANG! BANG! "Brother." BANG! BANG! "You fucking bitches." BANG! BANG! BANG! CLICK! He screamed at the top of his lungs, as he emptied the pistol and sped off, too wounded and surrounded to get to Shorty's body and get him in the truck. Shorty Slice was gone, and it was all Pretty Boy's fault.

As Pretty Boy fled the scene, flashbacks of the white Nissan Altima haunted him as he recalled seeing the car on Springfield Avenue near Vaux Hall. It was full of white bitches and also, he saw it across the parking lot in Miranda's townhouse complex. Now, Shorty Slice was dead. Pretty Boy had fucked up.

Chapter 9
Miami Massacre

After receiving some very vital news from one of his main bitches that worked at a hospital in Orlando, Florida, Tito had found out that Baby Hatchet was laying up there healing and had been there for a while under the name Richard Smith. She was certain it was him, down to the bullet wounds he suffered and the description Tito had given her from the photo. She further confirmed it after he sent her a picture of Baby Hatchet; it was a positive match, no doubt about it, he was there.

Speechless, Chinky, and Gorilla sat down with Tito at his Miami mansion and discussed the important information about Baby Hatchet, and their next moves. Speechless wanted it to be certain.

"Are you absolutely positive Tito, that this woman of yours is reliable in a situation like this brother? We need to be positive before we make a move because once we move on this, people will die, that's for sure. She described everything down to the bullet injuries huh? What about his machete tattoo? Did she get a chance to make that out since you have spoken with her?" Speechless asked Tito.

"She is legit brother, she is very legit and if she says he is there, trust me, he is there because she knows what type of man I am and she knows that I don't play fucking games Speechless. It's the real deal bro, he is there and we must act now! She didn't mention any tattoo yet, but she will bet her life on it that that's him for certain," Tito replied. "Are you guys ready?" he continued to inquire.

"Of course, we are. That's one of the reasons we stayed down here, to finish this shit once and for all. He has to be dealt with and erased from this fucking earth. We do this shit now!" voiced Gorilla, ignoring another call from Jamaica, who had been calling him the entire trip every hour on the hour, in his ear about leaving the game alone. He had gotten tired of hearing that shit every time he answered her call.

"Gorilla is right, we do this shit now!" expressed Chinky. "We kill this motherfucker for all the fallen soldiers in our family and any future plans he ever had of taking shit over once he re-emerges in New Jersey again because that's how motherfuckers like him think. Rebuild his Butcher Boys down here and resurrect something we have already destroyed up there, only to have it come back stronger and disguised as something else; something that we would never see coming! We have to get him now!" Chinky continued to express. Then his phone rung. "Excuse me brothers, got to take this," He said to the sit-down.

"I agree Speechless, act now and end this war that can plague your family's growth and future goals, we are here for you. You know this cannot happen, so therefore it isn't even a thought, you just act!" Tito said to his dear friend/half-brother. Speechless' phone then went off, then Gorilla's phone rang almost at the same time.

Then they could hear Chinky screaming into his phone before Speechless and Gorilla could answer theirs'.

"What the fuck? Where are you at brother? Who did what? Shorty Slice? What? Aw man no, that shit true bro. Say that that shit is not fucking true man. Hello! Pretty Boy! Tell me this shit not true man!" Chinky zapped out into the receiver, while Speechless and Gorilla rushed into the room with him, ignoring their own phone calls. Tito stood as well to check on them.

"Hello? Pretty Boy talk to me man. Fuck is up? Where Shorty Slice?" asked Speechless, after he had snatched the phone from a stunned Chinky's hand. "Pretty Boy what happened? Where are you and are you alright? Where the fuck is Shorty Slice at? What the fuck happened up there, what's going on?" he pressed Pretty Boy over the phone after seeing the tears streaming down Chinky's face uncontrollably, and watching him grab a chair and slowly sit down.

"Chinky, what the fuck man? Talk to me slanted-eyes. What the fuck happened up there brother, what's up?" barked Gorilla, but his question fell on deaf ears, as Chinky could not hear anything at that moment. One of his brothers had been killed, his comrade, his older confidant, gone.

"What! What the fuck do you mean Shorty Slice is dead? Who? How the fuck? What? The motherfucking Nigerians did this shit? Where are you right now? You safe?" Speechless continued to lose control of his temper and explode on the phone. "You get hit bad

Pretty Boy? What the fuck did the doctor say so far? Are you going to be alright until we get up there? Sit fucking tight man alright, god damn! I can't believe this fucking shit. When the fuck did this shit happen Pretty Boy?" pressed Speechless, as he watched Gorilla start crying and he himself, began to shed tears for their fallen brother Shorty Slice.

"It went down yesterday. Shit is all over the news, but there was nothing about Shorty Slice on the television bro, shit is strange," Pretty Boy managed to say.

"Alright, alright. You sit tight and rest up where you are until we get there you hear me bro?" asked Speechless.

"Yeah, I hear you Speechless," Pretty Boy replied.

"Are you sure he's dead Pretty Boy?" Speechless asked him, putting the phone on speaker.

"Yeah brother. They blew his face off. Motherfucking white bitches man, they came from nowhere," replied Pretty Boy.

Everyone in the room was stunned and completely shocked by the terrible news. Everyone except Speechless; he was enraged!

"Gorilla, you take Tony and Marko with you and handle this shit with Baby Hatchet immediately. Snatch his ass up out of there, do what the fuck you have to do. We have got to get back to Newark immediately. I want this motherfucker dead, pronto brother and I know you can get it done. All hell has broken loose up there with these vengeful ass Africans, they never let that shit with Uzi Malik slide, they never forgot," Speechless said.

"Consider it done. Tito, where are the guys and where's the information on this motherfucker? We need to go now?" Gorilla asked him about Marko and Tony's whereabouts and the hospitals' exact location, plus the ward he was hiding in.

"They will be here in ten minutes," replied Tito.

After Gorilla, Tony, and Marko left for Orlando, Speechless and Chinky said their goodbyes to Tito Calversero and promised to return soon for a more casual visit and vacation so that they could further discuss possible joint-ventures down in Florida. At the hanger for their and Tito's private jets, they exchanged handshakes and embraced. Then Speechless and Chinky boarded the jet, knowing that their brother Gorilla was going to handle shit with Baby Hatchet.

They were at Newark International Airport in less than three hours. All hell was getting ready to break loose up in Newark, New Jersey.

Meanwhile, in a private area of South Beach, Miami, another crew was plotting the demise of those responsible for the death of their dear ones.

Onyx, Amy, Peridot, and Jade were the leaders of the Diamond Dolls and the younger sisters of the slain Pocahontas Mamas but their entire Diamond Dolls Crew consisted of: Precious, Turquoise, Opal, Pearl, Sequin, Platinum, Silver, and Goldie as well. All twelve of them were just as deadly and beautiful as their big sisters and predecessors were because they were younger. Being younger had multiple advantages for them, and one of them was that fact that they always had something to prove because of where they came from and who had schooled them. People tend to think that they can take advantage of someone younger than them, thinking that they are easy to manipulate or persuade. Men always go for the younger women because older women have already been around the block once or twice so they feel they don't have to deal with someone who is already set in her ways of doing things; most of the time it's a headache. Younger women are most susceptible to change and being introduced to new things. Most are easily impressed by flamboyancy. These youngsters were a rare breed though; as mature as women in their 30's, and more street smart than a female who had spent ten years hustling and grinding in the hood. They were a force to be reckoned with.

"Paco tells me that the motherfuckers responsible for our loss ladies call themselves the 50/50 Crew. They are from out of Newark, New Jersey and they had drama with Paco's boss. Then B.H. hired our sisters to handle this big job; that bullshit at B & B's that cost our family their fucking lives last year!" voiced an angry Onyx, who was drop-dead gorgeous but her heart was a cold black one. She was just twenty-one years old, but she was very, very mature and experienced; a natural leader. She made sure that the Diamond Dolls made their mark in the state of Florida, and down south abroad: Atlanta, South Carolina, Virginia, Missouri, Louisiana, and North Carolina were all of the states on their hit list of accomplishments. Meaning those were the states they had run through putting in work.

"I want fucking revenge for my big sister. She can't even fucking walk or use the bathroom on her own. They fucked her up bad and every day she wishes she was dead along with her comrades in arms," Turquoise said about her sister Emerald, who was the only surviving Pocahontas Mama that survived the slaughter at B & B's strip club when five of them were killed along with (the former) Ms. Cuba, two of Baby Hatchet's personal guards, and three natives of New Jersey, two black males and a Puerto Rican female. The 50/50 Crew had left her crippled, with a permanent shit bag for the rest of her life, and her little sister was going to make sure that they paid with their lives.

"We know who they are, what's our next move Onyx?" asked Peridot, who was the younger sister of the slain Gemma.

"Yeah Onyx, how are we going to move on these millionaire ballers from up Jersey? We owe it to our teachers and fallen siblings to avenge them, but we don't want to make the same mistake they made or worse," said Jade, who was the baby sister of Diamond, one of the Pocahontas Mamas leaders.

"We aren't going to make the same mistake they made because we are going to be smarter in our approach girls. We are going to gain the confidence of someone close to them somehow. Then when they least expect it, we will kill them all!" said Amy, who was the younger sister of the twins Ruby and Sapphire of the Pocahontas Mamas that died along with Diamond, Gemma, and Topaz.

"Those motherfuckers are in for a serious fucking ride, that's for sure!" exclaimed Peridot, who was one dangerous little mama, and the baby sister of the once deadly Gemma of the infamous Pocahontas Mamas. "They don't know What the fuck they started, and they damn sure are not ready for what's coming!" she continued.

"We ride and we fucking die for ours ladies; nothing else to it. They violated our world by shedding the blood of our loved ones, so it is fucking imperative for us to return the favor, ten fold!" yelled Platinum, who was only nineteen, but had been in training since she was fifteen years of age. She was ruthless and cold-hearted after having her young heart broke already when she was just sixteen and in High School. She, Goldie, Silver, and Pearl were all first cousins and all the same age and they all were brought up in the game by

Diamond and Gemma.

"All we have to do is plant our pretty little selves up in New Jersey for a while, like say the whole Summer or Fall, and we do what we do best; book them hustlers and the big boys until we get to this 50/50 Crew, then we do them dirty my sisters!" said Opal, who was best friends with Onyx, and just as fucking black-hearted. She was five foot seven inches tall, weighed one hundred and sixty-five pounds, and had a killer body like the rest of her Diamond Dolls clique. They were all stunningly beautiful with the beach bodies to match. Any man was putty in their hands.

"No matter how long it takes, we will get these motherfuckers; millionaire gangsters or not. No man can resist the superstar bitches in this crew, no man!" voiced Sequin, who was older than everyone in the Diamond Dolls at twenty-four years of age. She was also the only blonde-haired Diamond Doll, which made her more attractive and noticeable whenever they were all out and about scoping the scene for potential sugar-daddies or victims. By the time she was twenty years old, she had already killed two men for money and she had two different guys spending major money on whatever she wanted. One was a married doctor from California that she met on the beach in Miami, and the other was a police sergeant, also married from out in Naples, Florida. She had milked them for all that she could before Diamond and Gemma made her set them up in blackmail scandals to which the Pocahontas Mamas and the Diamond Dolls split over a million dollars.

"All I know is this. If we don't kill these motherfuckers and avenge our sisters and mentors, we aint shit!" voiced Precious, finally speaking up after listening to everybody talk about what they were going to do. "We do this shit right and we won't have anything to worry about sisters, and once the plan is made, we stick to it! We don't get off track or try some different shit. If it takes us moving up there for a motherfucking year then that's what it takes. Pack up your motherfucking Gucci and Prada luggage because you know what, these cocksuckers are going to die for what they did to the legendary Pocahontas Mamas; my word on my life!" she concluded. She was a fiery red-head that decided to change the color of her hair to match her volcanic ways, her volatile temper, and her thirst for blood. She was the twenty-three year old big cousin of Jade, which meant that Diamond was her big cousin, as well as mentor. She was bow-legged and had almond-shaped eyes that got her over in life more times than many. The color of her eyes were bluish-green, and she carried herself like the bad bitch she was at 5ft. eight inches tall and 170 pounds.

"Right, exactly what I am saying sister!" said Jade. "Whatever the fuck we need to do!" she continued.

"Get ready to go on vacation if we don't get these motherfuckers in Florida ladies. Get ready for a long fucking vacation," said Onyx.

Gorilla, Marko, and Tony all reached the hospital in Orlando without incident and they were hot on the trail of Baby Hatchet, who thought that he was safely stashed away at this hospital. Even though he had paid the necessary people a lot of money for this comfort and privacy, it did not work because the wrong person saw him at the right time and he was exposed. Had it not been for Tito expressing his concern for this terrible person who had did his family a horrible injustice not too long ago while they ate dinner one evening, she probably never would have mentioned it at all. It was a terrible coincidence for Baby Hatchet, and an incredible turn of luck for Tito and the 50/50 Crew.

They all dressed as soda machine delivery guys and two of them carried clipboards, while Gorilla wheeled in a soda machine as though they were there to replace one of the machines on one of the hospitals' upper floors. The mock soda machine was provided by Tito, who had many different ways and methods if someone ever needed to be snatched or disposed of. The soda machine just had a "face" on it, which gave it the appearance of a legit soda machine, but it really was hollow on the inside and completely empty; big enough to store two grown bodies inside of it.

When they got up to the sixth floor, where Joanna said "Richard Smith" was being treated, they immediately saw her. Marko recognized her from her many visits to Tito's mansion in Miami. They already knew that she was working that night, and she was willing to assist Tito any way that she could. Besides the fact that he was a gangster and cold-blooded killer, she was in love with Tito. She saw Marko along with Tony and some giant black guy that was bent at the waist wheeling in a soda machine on a hand-truck, but was still gigantic. She knew that things were getting ready to get ugly in the high-security ward of the sixth floor, so she headed to the cafeteria and waited to be contacted if she was needed.

    Tony and Marko began to search the ward and private rooms, while Gorilla attempted to unload the soda machine from the trolley and started scanning the floor for Baby Hatchet as well. It didn't take them long to find him either. He was at the far rear of the ward, and he had taken up enough space for two patients with the accommodations provided to him. He was living like a fucking king with everything from satellite television, to custom meals that were delivered on a daily basis twice a day, and he must have had one of those big custom meals right before they arrived at the hospital because he was sound asleep. He had no goons or bodyguards protecting him, and there were no nurses in the immediate area because they had all been called away by their supervisor, Joanna, to come and help out with a serious liquid spill in the cafeteria area. Apparently, someone had accidentally knocked over a rack with fifteen pans of hot soup on it and caused a massive mess that stretched across a large portion of the floor. Altogether, it took eight nurses and two orderlies forty-three minutes to clean up the spill of vegetables and soup, and in that time, the three hit men had drugged Baby Hatchet, loaded him into the mock soda machine standing up, secured his body and fled the building with him. Two hours later, the hospital realized that patient Richard Smith had been abducted from the recovery ward without a trace, and there were no signs of a struggle.

    As soon as they arrived in Miami with Baby Hatchet, Speechless was notified and disposal instructions were given to Gorilla. He didn't need Tony and Marko for the task ahead of him, so they were let go because they had things to do and people to see.

    After years and years of bloodshed, countless wars, and slaughters of their enemies, Gorilla never could imagine doing anything else but making millions with his brothers his crew, and continuing to prosper. Yet here he was, with pressure from his soul mate Jamaica weighing heavy on him to leave the 50/50 Crew, a constant reminder of how close he came to losing her a few years ago when the 50/50 Crew was at war with the Butcher Boys over control of Essex County. The enemy goons had kidnapped and raped her, but she had managed to live after they had left her for dead and now, she wanted him out of the game, the game that made him "Gorilla". The game was in his veins, it had given him millions, plus success beyond his wildest dreams. He loved it all: the hustle, the muscle, the ability to intimidate the competition the profit the growth and bond within his team as responsible businessmen (both illegal and legal), every aspect of the game was a "drug" to Gorilla.

As he stood in the confines of a cellar, located at some secluded hideaway, Gorilla held a brand-new 16-guage shotgun to the head of a man strapped tightly to a chair with a gag in his mouth and a potato sack over his head.He gripped the shotgun with extremely strong hands and pumped a cartridge into the chamber of the deadly weapon...The eerie echo could be heard all over the enormous basement of Tito's mansion in Miami.Marko and Tony left Gorilla alone with the man, because they had other extremely important business to handle for Tito. The basement doubled as a torture chamber for obtaining information from the opposition and eventually, making bodies disappear...

"You killed my brothers you bitch-ass nigga!" barked Gorilla at the whimpering figure. You and your motherfucking people are responsible for causing my lady permanent damage pussy, and now it's time to pay the motherfucking piper bitch!" continued an angry Gorilla.

"Mmmmmmmmmmmmmm...." came the mumbles of the hooded and gagged captive. "Mmmmmmmmmmmmmmmmmm..." came the noises again from the whimpering, terrified person even louder this time.

"What? You fucking bitch!" Yelled an infuriated Gorilla, snatching off the potato sack and revealing a terrified and battered Baby Hatchet. "Shut all that motherfucking noise up playboy you know what time it is bitch! It's fucking curtains for you!" Gorilla barked, swinging the back of the shotgun in the direction of baby hatchet, connecting with his nose and shattering it completely. Baby Hatchet tried to yell out in pain, but his cries were stifled by the gag. Tears ran down his face as he pissed himself...

"I don't want to do this anymore!" he yelled out. "You killed my baby sister Dolly and threatened my family cocksucker but you will bring harm to no one else motherfucker!" he continued. "I don't want to do this shit anymore!" he yelled, even louder this time more emotional. Then, without hesitation he put the massive shotgun to the face of Baby Hatchet and rested the barrel on his smashed nose then he pulled the trigger, putting an end to the nemesis that plagued the 50/50 Crew for far too long.

Chapter 10
R. I. P.

When Speechless and Chinky got back home to Newark, New Jersey it was not the same. They were not happy to be home because one of their brothers and best friends had been murdered. Shorty Slice was a soldier, a partner, a gangster, a father, and once, a husband and he would be missed dearly by the many people he touched. His friends, his brothers in the 50/50 Crew would not rest until the people responsible for Shorty's death were all dead. There was nothing else to it, that's how they rolled with one another. You hurt one of mines, then I touch five of your people. You kill any boss affiliated with the 50/50 Crew, then your entire organization will eventually be destroyed! They were furious that the body of Shorty Slice was never recovered from the murder scene, and when they heard the news from Pretty Boy himself, both Speechless and Chinky was pissed the fuck off with him.

"What's the deal Pretty Boy? How are you holding up brother?" asked Speechless, as he and Chinky entered one of the 50/50 Crew secret stash houses that doubled as recovery quarters for injured members.

"Brother, it's good to see you, how are you doing man?" asked Chinky, giving Pretty Boy dap and a two-handed hug as Speechless did.

"Seen better days, that's for sure brothers. I can't believe he's gone man," Pretty Boy said, expressing his emotions.

"What the fuck happened out there in them streets while we were gone brother? How the fuck could something like this have happened Pretty Boy?" questioned Speechless.

"The Nigerians. They were still angry about the shit with Uzi Malik I guess, so they waited until we were divided by the Miami trip to attack us. They made a move on Shorty Slice six weeks ago, tried to ambush him on 16th Avenue near Westside Park but Shorty Slice killed both of them. One he ran over with the Audi truck, and the other he chased him down as he tried to cut through the park and shot him dead on 17th Avenue. We had to do something. They were killing our business by tens of thousands every week Speechless. We knew it was them because no one is foolish enough to fuck with any territories controlled by the 50/50 Crew! Once we organized a strike team and hit some of their main strips, they began to take a tremendous loss as our profits began to return to normal because Newark Police placed mobile sub-stations on every corner of the Nigerians that we hit. After the attempt on Shorty Slice's life, we hit them again, harder this time. We went after their women. Wives, girlfriends, and mistresses; we wanted to really hit them where it hurt!" stated Pretty Boy, with regret in his eyes.

"Are you fucking shitting me Pretty Boy? You motherfuckers KNOW that a move like that should not have happened without discussing it with the rest of your brothers first! That was a dumb move bro and the shit eventually cost Shorty Slice his fucking life. No wonder he is dead, you motherfuckers tried to take on the entire Nigerian organization by your motherfucking selves. I spoke with you on the phone and asked you was everything alright, and you told me everything was cool. Now we find out that you were keeping shit concealed from the family in order to what? To prove that you could do shit alone motherfucker? You are not alone! That's what we are for!" Speechless began to lose his temper and yell at Pretty Boy out of anger. "How the fuck could you even think to hide some shit like this from the 50/50 Crew Pretty Boy? Shit doesn't even make fucking sense!" he continued to scold him.

"I know I fucked up bad; got Shorty Slice killed. Damn, Shorty Slice! Can't believe you are gone big bro," Pretty Boy responded, crying uncontrollably, knowing that he really was responsible for this loss to the family.

"Brother, we have to make this right immediately Pretty Boy. We have to kill these motherfuckers for Shorty Slice man, fuck the dumb shit. Yeah, you fucked up bad but the Nigerian motherfuckers fucked up worse!" expressed Chinky, as he embraced Pretty Boy in a bear hug.

"You motherfucking right we are going to make this shit right right motherfucking now Pretty Boy, no more fuck-ups. This shit cannot happen again understand?" asked Speechless.

"Understood ,Speechless," Pretty Boy replied.

They lit up some sour diesel and smoked to the memory of their fallen brother Shorty Slice.

When the shoot-out was over with the 50/50 Crew members that The Chinchillas were hired to kill, six bodies lay dead: two of the 50/50 Crew's shooters, and four Caucasian women in their early twenties. Although seven people died in that gun battle, there was no body of Shorty Slice left behind, and no mention of it in the newspaper. It was as if his body just disappeared. The body of Shorty Slice did not disappear at all. It was taken by the Nigerians.

Hyena and Cheetah were down the street watching the job get carried out correctly from a minivan the whole time. That's when they saw the one they call Pretty Boy speeding off to avoid the hail of bullets coming towards his direction. After the Audi truck he was driving left the scene, they could see the other one that they had known as Shorty Slice fall to the ground, dead. Immediately they drove quickly down the street, got out and picked up his body, then they dumped him in the van and drove off. After checking on their fallen sisters in arms to see if anyone else had lived, the surviving Chinchillas labored off to the safety of the getaway car they had parked in that area the day before. The hit on the 50/50 Crew was not a success, it was a failure because not only did they not kill both targets, but they lost four members of their elite team; four irreplaceable bitches.

Once the Nigerians had reached their hideout with the body of Shorty Slice, they immediately took the corpse inside and down to the basement. They threw the limp body onto a table that looked as though its sole purpose for creation was to assist in the dismemberment and dissection of dead bodies.

His body was stripped down of all clothing and valuables, but he wasn't given a cleansing. Instead, Lion and Leopard entered the basement carrying very huge knives that were razor-sharp. They looked like small machetes. Leopard walked up close to the table where Shorty Slice's body lay. He took out a smaller carving knife from his waistband, and began to remove Shorty Slice's heart from his chest. He looked down at Shorty Slice's face but could see only the lifeless eyes of a dead man staring up at him as he sliced, carved, and dug into Shorty Slice's chest cavity and cut out his heart violently. When he was done, he held the heart of Shorty Slice high into the air, gore and tissue oozing slowly down his wrist and forearm as he did so.

"This is what happens to muddafuckas dat stand in our way bruddas. We get rid of dem but first we remove their hearts, their balls, and their fucking heads!" Barked Leopard, as he looked to Lion and at the same time they began to hack at Shorty Slice's neck with the huge knives until his head was sawed off completely. "Eat your fucking heart out muddafuckas," concluded Leopard, as he held Shorty Slice's heart in his left hand, and the bloody knife in the other. After carving up Shorty Slice's body, leaving nothing but the torso, Leopard took his head, his heart, and his balls and left the room leaving everyone to gloat over their victory.

The two remaining Chinchillas were devastated. Although he knew that his brothers were concerned and disappointed that they did not get both of the gang members, he himself was very proud of the hit, though he would not let his brothers know this. He knew from the news reports and the accounts of the surviving Chinchilla bitches, that two other guys from the 50/50 Crew also died, as well as four of the white bitches who were also declared dead at the scene. The two remaining bitches would get another chance to redeem themselves and try the assassination again but first he had to verbally chastise them for their failure. The death of one of the 50/50 Crew's bosses was a testament that they could be touched! Leopard was proud indeed. Now their slain women could rest in peace.

Dandelion, Dandi, and Tulips or two-lips were the only remaining Chinchillas left and after their meeting with the head of the Nigerians, they were more focused than ever. Leopard told them flat out that the only reason they were still alive after their failure was because they suffered significant loss to the murder squad he sent, and they were the only two remaining to finish the job. He assured them that if they failed again, that they might as well keep it moving and leave the country because clearly there would be big prices on their heads all across the states.

SWITCH HITTER 2: 50/50 Crew: 'Til Death Do Us

They knew better than to try and cross the Africans. They saw the mutilated body of Shorty Slice on that table. Leopard and Lion made the girls watch. They did consider themselves lucky because of the fact that they were not only wearing bullet-proof vests like their sisters had on, but that they didn't suffer a head or neck shot like the ones that ended the lives of their partners. As they regrouped, they plotted and waited for the right opportunity to strike the 50/50 Crew.

When Gorilla got back to Newark, New Jersey after the successful annihilation of Baby Hatchet, one of the 50/50 Crew's most wanted enemies, he had no idea what drama and bad news he was coming back to. He saw his wife Jamaica immediately because she was there at the hangar to pick him up and whisk him home before his boys had a chance to get him away on some type of business. As soon as he got in the car she started with him.

"Winston, what is the deal with you? You ignored most of my phone calls during your vacation and you deliberately didn't call me during your flight home! You are being so fucking disrespectful to me and you have never done me wrong or mistreated me. Tell me something damn it!" Jamaica demanded.

"Tell you something. Tell you something huh? I will fucking tell you something you ungrateful motherfucker! How dare you come at me like this Jamaica! I have never cheated on you in our lives. I have sacrificed my very being to make sure that you want for nothing. Yet you act as if my mission to rectify this drama with my brothers and me is not fucking important!

"My brothers and my 50/50 Crew family are the most important things to me in this world, they are my immediate family. Anything or anyone that I love in this world come secondary to that! Do you understand me woman? I don't want a woman at my fucking side for the rest of my fucking life that does not understand that we are very grown and quite mature, so we do not have to beat around the bush or waste time looking for possibilities Jamaica, it is what it is baby. God damn. I met you and Kelvin the same motherfucking day and you two saved me from the same motherfucking group of thugs. Then I went on to become Gorilla, and at the side of Speechless, Chinky, Pretty Boy, and Shorty Slice, who just so happen to have gotten himself murdered the other day by the way. I have killed many and made millions in the process of building and maintain our 50/50 Crew empire. I love those motherfuckers and would give my life for them without question because they would do the same for ME over and over if they had to.

"So, you see, it was fucking imperative that I went on vacation and handled that business involving my crew, because motherfuckers violated and you were kidnapped. Uzi Malik, both Twins, and Dolly all dead. My brother Chinky almost died as he lay wounded from gunshots from the same motherfuckers that snatched you. It was my motherfucking duty and obligation as one of the leaders of this family to make sure that those responsible answered for their violations to my family. Do you understand that?" He continued to express himself as they drove to the mini-mansion they occupied together out in West Orange.

She was crying as he went on and on. She had no idea that Shorty Slice was dead. It stunned her when he had said that, and everything else was pretty much muffled to her ears after that.

"I hear what you are saying. Sorry about your friend. I didn't know about Shorty Slice. I have loved you unconditionally since the very first time we met and chose each other, but I want you out of this game Gorilla, fuck that! I have a right to be selfish and demand that much from my man, my husband! I too have sacrificed my goals and dreams to be the wife of a hustler, but this shit has grown tired and fucking dangerous Winston. I thought you would have got out of the game after they kidnapped me and raped me for Christ's sake but here you are, still getting money and traveling from state-to-state handling business.

I have gone everywhere and done everything for you, without asking a motherfucking question. I have played my part as the loving and caring and supportive wife but it has just become too much for me baby, and I can't take being under so much stress all of the time! It's easy for you, you're a gangster, so the violation of life and exploitation of the city means nothing to you, I understand that. I have even grown to embrace it, but I cannot live my life like this anymore. I'm sorry," Jamaica said to him as she drove with tears running down her face.

"So am I Jamaica. It's over between us, we are done," Gorilla responded emphatically, cracking the passenger window and sucking in the much-needed air.

After the 50/50 Crew all got together, they had to plan the homegoing service for Shorty Slice and begin to plot their revenge for the loss to their family. The service would be private of course, and only the closest of friends and family were notified as to the details of the ceremony. They were all at one of their newest clubs, way back in the rear discussing this serious plan of execution.

"We have to hit and hit them hard!" said Chinky opening up the floor.

"We cannot let this shit slide in any way, shape, or form brothers. We kill every single last one of those Nigerian motherfuckers and anyone attached to them. This is all out motherfucking war! They killed Shorty Slice, and that's just like any one of us getting murdered in this room right now, and I already know everyone here now would give his very last breath for the man sitting next to him," voiced Gorilla.

"That is the obvious. We have no other choice. We are the 50/50 crew, and if you violate one of us, you die!" Speechless spoke up.

"Not only do the Nigerians have to die, those hired white bitches must go too! Right along with the coward-ass Nigerians. All of them motherfuckers must die!" Pretty Boy spoke up.

"These motherfuckers killed Shorty Slice man. Shorty fucking Slice. Just can't believe this shit y'all, our brother is fucking gone! The streets will run bloody for months until we gun all of those bitches the fuck down!" blurted out Chinky.

"Yeah, they asses are dead for sure," Speechless said, lighting up one in the memory of Shorty Slice and smoking it to himself.

They held the ceremony privately as planned, and because there was no body to put into the coffin or anything to display at the viewing, they just placed a giant urn on the mantel that was halfway full with ashes from a fireplace somewhere. It was told to everyone concerned that Shorty Slice had to be cremated because of the headshots and damage to his face. The 50/50 crew still had not yet recovered his body.

After the service ended and all of the family members and close friends left the parking lot safely, the 50/50 Crew headed towards one of their arsenal stashes to grip up for the sudden war that was getting ready to hit the streets of Newark, New Jersey. They had lost a very dear friend and brother but many families would suffer for what the Nigerians started. A lot of motherfuckers were getting their expiration dates early!

Every one of the 50/50 Crew swore vengeance on the Nigerians for the deaths of their comrades. Especially their big brother Shorty Slice. Armed with automatic rifles, high-caliber handguns, a few twenty-five automatic silenced pistols, a lot of concussion, flash, and fragment grenades, ten automatic shotguns, and a stinger. They each wore a titanium box-cutter on their belts to the memory of the deceased Shorty Slice, and for up close and personal combat!

The 50/50 Crew agreed that they wouldn't waste another day. They would hit the Nigerians anywhere and everywhere they were at any moment of the day or night. They would get it done before Pretty Boy's sisters' wedding to Diablo.

The Nigerians went about business as usual after the murder of Shorty Slice and they didn't fear retaliation, they were ready for it, or so they thought. They were making more money than ever after re-establishing the necessary areas that needed conquering and a steady supply of raw heroin. They bought new cars, each vehicle boasting the colors of the Nigerian flag, to let everyone know what it was with them. They were not hiding at all!

One by one, twenty shooters and the remaining leaders of the 50/50 Crew got into five different customized mini-vans; bullet-proof, bomb-proof, and equip with run-flat tires as well. The van-tanks were all black and they were headed in a convoy towards the Ironbound Section (South Newark), where the Nigerians generated millions in months of off their raw brand of dope, and their dope houses down there.

Earlier that same morning, the very same day that the 50/50 Crew was preparing to execute their plan of revenge, Cheetah and Hyena were on their way back from delivering a special package to one of the 50/50 Crew leaders' address. The two packages were postmarked West Africa, no name attached, only a phony business address for return mail purposes. They drove a fake rush mail delivery service truck, and when Cheetah delivered the package to the front door, he was dressed head to toe in uniform and appeared to be a worker of that particular company. He just rang the doorbell twice and sat the packages on the front steps of Officer Patricia Grimes, the fiancée of the 50/50 Crew leader Speechless, then he vaulted down the short flight of front steps and they left the scene to go check their main trap houses.

Speechless drove the lead vehicle as the deadly caravan headed across McCarter Hwy and under the overpass. He was more focused than he had been on many other past missions before. He wanted retribution as he did when Salvatore and Tanya were murdered. Rivers of blood would flood the sewers of Newark for months. He parked diagonally across the street from their biggest dope house in that area three houses away, and retrieved the stinger from the side entrance of the minivan. Then, as the other vehicles sped by to attack the other blocks down there that the Nigerians owned, he squeezed the trigger of the missile launcher and sent an explosive torpedo directly at Nigerians' dope house! From the first floor on up the house just exploded, causing chaos and mayhem on the busy dope strip and sending everyone running frantic, as the 50/50 Crew gunned down anyone resembling a hustler in the immediate area.

Hyena and Cheetah were both inside the dope house collecting the weekly profits when the missile came through the window. Then everything was eternally dark for them.

Speechless stood there for a few seconds after the house blew up, just watching it collapse in a pile of rubble and fire, while gunfire erupted everywhere around him. He was thinking about Shorty Slice. A bullet whizzed by his left ear, as Nigerian and Afro-American drug dealers scrambled for cover and survival all over. Before Speechless could even react to the shooter, someone from the 50/50 Crew gunned him down then kept it moving in the violent assault on the Nigerian crew. Speechless dipped and ducked to the side of the minivan, then placed the stinger back where it belonged, and grabbed an automatic pump shotgun so that he could join in on the slaughter.

He went for nothing but upper chest and head shots with the pump, blowing motherfuckers faces off because they represented an organization that he was soon going to destroy. He caught at least four people and laid them flat. There was no coming back from the deadly accurate blows he delivered. Then he ran across the street and down the block to assist Pretty Boy, Chinky, and Gorilla because they were chasing and gunning on at least twenty motherfuckers from that block, who must have went and gripped up for war because now all of a sudden some of them had heart.

As Speechless charged the crowd, he could see Gorilla shooting somebody in the side of the head and another one quickly in the forehead. A third charged Gorilla, but was cut down when a blast from the shotgun Speechless held blew his legs off at the knees. Chinky was there on point and shot the same shooter in the back of the head as he struggled with his weapon and tried to grasp at his legs that were no longer there. Pretty Boy was in the middle of slicing someone's throat after he clearly had ran out of ammunition during the battle and was too far away from any of the vans to get another firearm. Then he turned just in time to catch one of the Africans in mid-swing with a machete, dodged the attempt at his head and slashed the goon across the face as Gorilla came, grabbed the dude from behind, and cut into his throat with the boxer cutter. Blood sprayed everywhere, then the limp body dropped.

Chinky was running up the steps to one of the Nigerian dope houses busting shots with two 9mm Berettas, which held seventeen shots a piece and kicked in the front door easily because of the goons they had in place on the stairs, they didn't even keep the door locked. Chinky had shot and fatally wounded at least five of the six Nigerian thugs that were sitting on the porch, and when he got inside the dope house he just kept on shooting until the slide came back and the gun was empty. Then, as he backed out his razor when he heard more gunshots and yelling near him, Speechless walked up to him and handed him a forty aliber.

"Here, take this Chinky and let's finish these motherfuckers. Make them fucking shots count!" BANG! Speechless said, as he shot another enemy fleeing for the open door.

"Thanks brother, and you know that I am a better fucking shot than you!" BANG! BANG! BANG! BANG! Chinky said, as he took aim and shot two more of the Africans' shooters, giving them two shots each; chest and face shots.

"Let's get this shit done and move on to the next goldmine they have for us to destroy. We want nothing but blood. Let the soldiers get the spoils," Speechless said.

"Okay then, you ready I'm ready, let's finish this business," said Chinky, as they went through the house killing who they could and still, wasn't satisfied because they knew that they hadn't gotten the leaders of the Nigerian crew. They would find out later on that day, that they had in fact slain three of the top dogs in the enemy camp.

After the destruction of the Nigerians turf down the Ironbound Section, the 50/50 Crew grouped up and prepared to hit some of the other spots and areas the Africans controlled. Then all of a sudden, Speechless got a call from his wife Patricia.

"Hello, baby I can't talk right now. Very important shit is going on and I-," before he could get out another word, she abruptly cut him off, screaming at the top of her lungs into the receiver and his ear!

"The motherfucking bastards! They mailed his heart, balls and his damn head to the fucking house! I went to open up the damn box because its addressed to the both of us! Poor Shorty Slice! They cut off his head Kelvin! They cut off his heart, and they cut off his manhood! What kinds of animals are you dealing with out there?" She screamed into the phone at Speechless but he was numb. The last thing he heard her say, was 'Poor Shorty Slice.'

"What? Sit tight woman. I will be right there in a minute! Calm down and stop fucking screaming in my ear!" Speechless yelled over the phone at a hysterical Patricia. "I will be there shortly baby, hold tight okay!" he concluded, hanging up the phone to stop the minivan so that he could give his crew new orders on which areas to take out and destroy while he took care of something very important and urgent.

Everyone that was in the minivan with Speechless got into the one that Gorilla was in and then Gorilla got into the minivan with Speechless and they sped off heading for Routes one & nine.

When they arrived at Speechless and Patricia's house, they could see her sitting on the porch sobbing uncontrollably with her knees up to her breast and her arms around her knees. They quickly reached her side and Speechless helped her up and into his arms then into the house and then he smelled the stench and saw the boxes on the floor. The son of a bitch had decapitated and castrated his brother Shorty Slice and on top of that, they cut out his heart and packages it all up, just to ship to him! The gall of those motherfuckers! He swore on his life at that moment that this shit would never end as long as one of those African pussies were living and breathing. He would hunt them all down no matter how long it took!

"Motherfuckers! Holy shit, Shorty Slice!" exclaimed Gorilla, when he saw the mutilated body of his fallen comrade. "You motherfuckers are going to die horribly. He swore every fucking last one of you!" Gorilla continued, standing over the body parts of Shorty Slice that were still in the opened boxes sprawled across the floor.

"They are going to wish that they were never born," replied Speechless, as he and Gorilla gathered the three packages together and left the house with a shaken Patricia.

Chapter 11
Kill Everything

The day of the raid on the Nigerians and the day that Shorty Slice's remains were found, was the day the 50/50 Crew decided that they would indefinitely eliminate the entire Nigerians crew. From the lowest level runner that worked for them, all the way up to the boss of bosses. They would all perish at the hands, knives, or bullets of the 50/50 crew.

After Speechless had taken Patricia to a safe spot and made sure she was going to be good for at least the rest of the week, he summoned his 50/50 Crew and set out again on another murderous assault. They went all over Newark where they knew that the Nigerians had heroin jumping and they killed everyone. Block after block, dope house after dope house. They imposed their deadly presence and left no one alive unless they were hiding somewhere and didn't make a sound. They blew up all of the known businesses ran or owned by their African rivals, and they didn't spare any C4 either. The entire store, car dealership, or any other business they owned was completely destroyed beyond repair or refurbishment. They were being obliterated financially and whenever one or two of them were seen in public, the necessary shooters were notified and they were killed on site, whether broad daylight or during the night. Anyone caught flagging their colors or driving the cars they drove or loaned to relatives, were also murdered. The 50/50 Crew wasn't playing any games and they squeeze was on in the vast city of Newark, New Jersey to get rid of the people responsible for killing Shorty Slice, and their other shooters.

The Nigerians wanted to get immediate revenge for the violent deaths of their family members, but there was no time for retaliation, only retreat. The 50/50 Crew were applying pressure with full-force and members of their organization were dying at every turn, plus all of their businesses were gone or being targeted for destruction. Over fifteen businesses gone within a week and almost one hundred murders since the war began. With the heat just around the corner, the remaining leaders of the Nigerian crew had decided to head back home for a year to lay low, wash their millions, and regroup later on in the states somewhere else, possibly Boston or Upstate New York maybe.

"Dis shit is far from ova muddafukas. We will see you bitches again, and then you can join your partner Shorty Slice!" said Lion out loud, so that the rest of his entourage could hear his rant. Then, he asked the remaining Chinchillas to join him and his entourage in West Africa for the year or so that they would be gone. They reluctantly accepted his offer, they knew that he was not asking.

They were leaving the United States for West Africa in two weeks.

As the murders increased in various areas within and surrounding Newark, police presence was also increased tremendously and Patricia was concerned for her man and his team. She wanted him to take his businesses elsewhere and expand in another geographical area altogether. She wanted him to be smart and outlast any of the people she had known that didn't make it in "the life." She wanted him to get out of Newark. She knew that Kelvin would avenge his dear friend Shorty slice, and she knew that it would end very, very bloody.

As the Nigerians prepared for their return home, the 50/50 Crew hit the streets for information about the Nigerians and their known affiliates. They were bent on retaliation and retribution and there wasn't anything or anyone that was going to stand in their way of killing the Nigerian crew. Speechless, Gorilla, Pretty Boy, and Chinky had paid a substantial amount of money to speak with Chop-Chop, a notorious snitch that had defected from the Nigerians crew four years prior because he had stolen over 1000 grams of pure heroin from them, with the hidden agenda to start his own organization using the same dope connections back home that Lion and the rest of them used. They had captured him and tortured him by cutting off his left hand with a machete, slicing into him deeply across his shoulders, legs, and back and just when they were going to kill him, the safe house was raided by the narcotics division task force on a tip from someone that the Nigerians had manufactured their dope packages there.

Two Nigerian soldiers were killed in a brief gun battle with the officers and two more were arrested for the kidnapping, torturing, and attempted murder of Oleban "Chop-Chop" Nyungo that night. After he had healed up and laid low for about ten months after his kidnapping and attempted murder, Chop-Chop reemerged and crept on the scene lurking in the shadows and on the outskirts at night, while his Nigerian counterparts shined and flossed every day in the public eye, washing their heroin profits through car dealerships and various other legitimate businesses. The hatred that Chop-Chop had for the Nigerian crew was beyond definition, it was beyond personal, it was stronger than mere revenge. It was a vindictive retribution that ran deep within him. Every time that he looked into the mirror or tried to wash himself, he was reminded of what they did and how they were still on top in the dope game in Newark.

More than anything, Speechless and the rest of his brothers in the 50/50 Crew always kept their word. If they said that they were going to do something, then it was done and if they said they were going to pay you for information then they paid you for your information and spared you your life. They were direct, not grimy, whenever they did business. When they met with Chop-Chop and his little henchmen, they exchanged information for money and there wasn't much said between the two parties except for when Speechless took the large envelope, and said to Chop-Chop,

"This shit better be the real deal Chop. We don't play games as grown motherfucking men. That's five hundred thousand dollars in that duffle for you. You take it easy and stay off the streets for a while," Speechless told him.

"I will take it easy and we wouldn't even be here if it wasn't all authentic and valuable info, I hate doze muddafuckas!" replied a bruised, battered, and ruined Chop-Chop, as he unzipped the duffel bag and examined the many bundles of ten- and twenty-dollar bills. The 50/50 Crew exited the meeting place and got into their bullet-proof customized conversion van. Once they started pulling out of the warehouse at a quick pace and were about twenty feet away from the meeting place, Chinky looked at Speechless for the signal.

"Now Chinky, do it!" Speechless said. Chinky then pressed the button on a remote-control he held, that was wired to an explosive package hidden under the pay-off money in the duffle bag and the warehouse's interior irrupted into flames and smoke, instantly killing everyone inside. There were too many witnesses, too many people saw their faces.

The information proved to be very valuable indeed and the 50/50 Crew was able to obtain the addresses and locations of the top members in the Nigerian organization, as well as the whereabouts of their lodges. The ones that didn't get switch around since Chop-Chop had crossed them some years ago. The envelope had pictures of all bosses, their families here in the states, their homes as well as the addresses and of course the addresses and locations of their hideouts.

Nobody could understand how or why the deaths came so quickly and violently, but the explanation wasn't necessary. It was revenge for the death of Shorty Slice, and the 50/50 Crew showed no mercy whatsoever. They gave the order to spare no one down to the motherfucking maid and the dog. They wanted everybody exterminated!

Day after day, door after door was kicked in suddenly, and bullets came from everywhere until there was no more screaming and yelling, until everyone in the residence or business was dead.

The leaders of the 50/50 Crew dispatched one hundred shooters and trained killers to ten different locations of the Nigerian crew, ten gunners each location and they were very efficient in carrying out the orders given by their bosses. They were shot in the heart and head, then the entire place was burned to the ground. They handled every hit in this manner, and they knew that failure was not an option because this was retaliation for one of their fallen leaders.

As the rest of the 50/50 Crew's soldiers put work in and carried out hits on the businesses and families of the Nigerian crew's leaders, the bosses of the 50/50 Crew, Speechless, Chinky, Gorilla, and Pretty Boy were headed towards the main hideout of the Nigerians. The secluded and secure place that they thought no one knew about. The 50/50 Crew was stealth in two twin Dodge Challengers equipped with all the specifics that were pretty much standard when it came to any of the bosses vehicles in the 50/50 Crew. They didn't play around when it came to security. They didn't take any chances at all! Now, here they were armed like a small army in pursuit of this clique of Africans that killed their man Shorty Slice, their brother.

"Listen, Pretty Boy. This is how you make it right brother. This is how you correct the mistake you made in allowing them white bitches to get the drop on you and Shorty Slice, rest in peace. You make these motherfuckers pay for what they did, and what they had intended to do to you as well, do you hear me bro? None of these motherfuckers live, not one soul. Not one motherfucking soul!" expressed Speechless.

"I hear you brother, and I know they can't live no way, no how. Lock and fucking load!" yelled Pretty Boy.

"Kill my motherfucking brother, cut his head off and take out his heart! Nah motherfuckers. You are going to truly know the wrath of the 50/50 Crew when this shit is over!" yelled Speechless into the windshield as he drove the super-fast muscle car towards the hidden hideout of the Nigerians. Meanwhile, Gorilla and Chinky were in the car behind them riding close because they knew that they were getting closer to their destination, and no one really knew if they were coming out of this alive or not. What they did know for certain was that none of the Africans were going to survive what was coming their way!

"Are all weapons locked and loaded Chinky? Make sure bro, because a split second or a weapon jamming could cost a nigga his fucking life in a gunfight my brother?" asked Gorilla.

"Yeah man I already know, and shit is fucking ready to go. Everything is secure Gorilla. All we got to do is fucking get there and it's the fourth of fucking July out here in Livingston! We got silencers on the pistols and suppressors on the big shits my brother, nobody fucking survives this shit Gorilla! None of those bitches either Gorilla, they took Shorty Slice away from us man and did him fucking dirty, so we have to return the favor and I brought my scalpels with me!" continued Chinky, with a menacing grin on his face.

"Motherfuckers are dead!" barked Gorilla, as he mashed down on the gas to keep up with Speechless and Pretty Boy, the car hugging the S-curves that cut through South Mountain Reservation.

They drove for about ten more minutes before some dark back roads and odd twists and turns brought them to a clearing. Chop-Chop's information was true, this was where the Nigerians had hid out for all these years and plotted and planned takeovers in the city of Newark, and the county of Essex. They could see numerous cars, including two limos and two original Hummers. Then they saw the guards posted all over the place and they were armed with A-R 15s and Uzi submachine guns, the place was enormous. Once they saw that, Speechless and Gorilla turned their cars around so that they could have an easier getaway, and parked about a quarter mile from the lodge so that they could strap-up and move out towards the compound. Each of them were now armed with at least two silenced pistols and a large fully-automatic rifle equipped with a sound suppressor, as well as one or two other concealed weapons. They had two clips a piece for the Berettas and 45s, and the big guns held the interchangeable quad-clip, that was actually four fifty-count clips welded together making the deadly weapon eligible to be reloaded up to four times without reaching for ammo or slowing down. They wore no mask, only bullet-proof vest with groin and neck protection. No one inside of the hide-out would live through this hit anyway, so they decided against any kind of masks. They only wore night-vision goggles. Once they were squared away and had checked then re-checked their artillery, they hauled ass towards the headquarters of the Nigerians with blood in their eyes and hatred in their hearts.

They quickly descended upon the lodge, and the armed guards had no clue whatsoever as to the deadly imminence amongst them.

One by one, body after body began to drop, as the 50/50 Crew made each shot count for something, connecting with deadly blows each time one of their bullets struck the enemy. Within a matter of fifteen minutes, they had managed to kill twelve guards and four vicious attack dogs. They moved as one unit, making sure that they didn't separate which would have made them more vulnerable. There was strength in numbers. When the attack dogs had been released, Speechless was ready for them as he pulled the pin on two grenades and tossed them one by one in the direction of the charging K-9s.

They found the rear entrance, and Gorilla quickly dismantled the guard that was standing in front of the door by sneaking up on him from the side and snapping his frail neck, then dragging his body into the woods.

Once the rear was cleared, Chinky picked the locks on the door and they entered the vast corridor to the lodge, and they could see that the Nigerians had to a lot of money into their hideout. They had lined the walls with expensive paintings and the hallways with rare sculptures that were easily worth hundreds of thousands of dollars. They were all inside now, and Pretty Boy, who was last to enter, made sure that the door was closed and then locked again, so that it would appear as though no one ever entered through there.

Walking apprehensively down the corridor, they were in a formation that preventing anyone from getting to them and taking them out. Gorilla was in the front of them, looking like something out of the Terminator movie the way he led the way with that big fully-automatic M-60 in front of him. Chinky had his gun aimed at the noises coming from the inside of the walls to the left of them, Pretty Boy had his gun trained on the voices coming from the walls to the right of them, and Speechless was covering the rear, holding the team down so that no one could take them by surprise once the bodies were discovered. Then the yelling started.

From out of nowhere specific, they could hear yelling and running, and the loading and cocking of weapons very close to them. The sound was coming right through the walls.

"Stop everybody, stop moving now!" ordered Speechless.

"What is it Speechless?" asked Gorilla, stopping in his tracks instantly and tensing up his body ready for confrontation.

"The walls. Everybody shoot through these motherfucking walls and kill everything!" Speechless yelled as he turned to the right and emptied two of the clips through the walls and into the soldiers that were standing on the other side strapping up for war. Then he swayed to the left and did the same thing, hitting a couple of troops that were also arming themselves. After briefly spacing themselves in the massive corridor, every one of the 50/50 Crew began to shoot through the walls, shredding them down to the thin wooden boards that held the sheetrock in place. They could see Africans scattering on the other side through the gigantic holes that were in the walls now, and they could see that some of them were trying to shoot back. Piles and piles of large caliber empty shells were stacking up in the hallway, then just when they were killing all of the African gangsters and had them on the run, Lion and Tiger appeared at opposite ends of corridor with flamethrowers attached to a shoulder strap. As soon as Speechless caught a glimpse of the hardware they were packing, he let off four shots at Lion, who was the nearest to him and hit him in the face.

"Look out Gorilla, in front of you!" Speechless yelled.

"Go through the walls, let's get better cover!" yelled Chinky.

"Watch out Rilla!" yelled Pretty Boy, as Gorilla shot a charging Tiger three times but didn't finish him right away, therefore allowing Tiger to get off a good squeeze of his flamethrower. The flames temporarily blinded Gorilla's vision and scorched him severely in the face. Most of the flames were blocked to a degree by the goggles, turtle-neck vest, and clothes that he wore that night, but he was very badly burned. Quickly Pretty Boy rushed to his aid, shooting Tiger in the face and chin finishing him for good and then he threw down his gun and lurched onto the front of Gorilla to smother the flames that were eating at his clothes. His lips, his chin, and his ears would be badly burned and permanently scarred for life but he would survive. As soon as the flames were out Gorilla tried to speak out,

"Get offfff me Prretty Boyyyy. I'm alright, I'm okay," He spat out through burned, blistered, and swollen lips. "Where Chinky at Ssppeechlesss? Are they alright?" Gorilla continued to inquire about his brothers.

"We are right here brother, we are good are you alright big guy?" asked Chinky, going over to stand with Gorilla and check on him.

"We are good Gorilla. All these bitches are dead except the ones that ran and got away, and this bitch ass motherfucker right here all shot up and shit! Bitch I am far from being done with your motherfucking ass Lion. Yeah I know who the fuck you are pussy and you can thank Chop-Chop for this one motherfucker!" barked an angered Speechless, as he stood over top off the body armor wearing Lion, who had been injured by two of the four shots Speechless had hit him with. "This is for Shorty Slice and Gorilla motherfucker!" said Speechless as he powerfully swung the icepick downwards into Lion's left eye. Lion screamed out in agonizing pain. He couldn't talk because of the gunshot wound to the face. Then again into his right eye, piercing the back of his skull and penetrating the floor. Then he picked up the flamethrower from the ground and threw the strap around his shoulder, bracing with the deadly weapon over Lion. Then out of nowhere Pretty Boy pushed Speechless to the side with his latex glove-clad hands, reached down Lion's pants with his left hand and with the small scalpel in his right hand he violently cut off Lion's dick then shoved it in his gaping mouth. After that, he stated to Lion,

"This is for my brother you bitch–ass motherfucker!" Pretty Boy screamed at him enraged.

"Watch Gorilla Pretty Boy. Get him. Move out the way for a second," Chinky said to his brother, as he took out a Glock-40 from one of his shoulder holsters and shot the already dead Lion point blank in the forehead. After that, Speechless closed the deal by standing only three feet away from Lion as he torched him face first for two minutes, then his body and his lair. Lastly, Speechless threw the flamethrower and two grenades into the fire, as the 50/50 Crew fled to their awaiting cars and their next mission rushing Gorilla to University.

As Speechless and the rest of the 50/50 Crew raced to get their badly wounded brother to the Burn Center at the Trauma Unit, the Nigerians hideout burned fiercely within the depths of the woods, and two people, were still alive within the flames. The two remaining Chinchillas, Dandelion and Tulips, who were both using the bathroom when the first burst of machine gun fire rang out, were still alive because they ran from the bathroom and hid inside of a giant old bank vault that the Africans kept as a safe inside of the wall. The safe was being cleaned that day and it left slightly ajar when all of the chaos and commotion started, and shooters ran back and forth trying to dodge bullets that were coming through the walls. They were ready to emerge from their shelter and had begun to slowly push open the vault door when they heard the two loud booms and felt the room shake. When they approached the safe door and peeped through the slit, they saw fire, smoke, and falling plaster, and wood. They knew right then and there that they had to get the hell out of there fast! As they made their way through the cold of the woods, they vowed that if they ever lived through this ordeal, that they would surely get revenge one day for their fallen sisters and they would once again, be The Chinchillas.

When the driver of the luxurious sedan stopped in the middle of the road that night at the sight of the half-naked, and apparently wounded young lady, he had no clue that his good deed would in fact cost him his life. For a week after they had taken him, the two remaining Chinchillas drained his bank accounts for all that they could, then they killed the dentist, torched his car and body, and fled back to Canada with a rented van full of merchandise of all kinds.

Meanwhile, Gorilla recovered with Jamaica by his side and all was forgiven as he realized that he didn't have the time to find his "perfect lady" all over again, it was Jamaica all along. She was it; the one he would make his wife for life. His brothers in the 50/50 Crew were always visiting him as he healed up, and skin-graft surgery after skin-graft surgery was performed on him to bring him back close to normal appearance. They were still in the streets taking care of business as usual, dealing with those that had to be dealt with, and getting ready for Pretty Boy's sisters' wedding to Diablo.

Chapter 12
Juniors' Return

As Joey Canelli Jr. sat in a maximum-security federal prison somewhere in Wisconsin, he contemplated his merciless takeover of all the New Jersey crime families and the ultimate revenge of killing whoever was responsible for the death of his dear Grandfather, the Don.

He hadn't had any problems since he was transferred from Kansas, where the Black Gorillas tried to bring an early end to his young Italian life. It was retaliation for the many Blacks that had been tormented at the hands, bats, knives, or guns of some Italian goon that threatened, assaulted, or killed their lives. They had him. He was trapped in a corridor on his way from a medical trip at the institutional clinic, with just one officer as an escort, when four huge Black convicts rushed him bearing jailhouse shanks. When the officer saw the threat he immediately pulled his emergency distress pin on his walkie-talkie and drew his stun-gun. He was able to hit two of the advancing thugs, but before he could do anything further he was stabbed in the neck, left eye, and the left side of his head; the last blow ending his life instantly. While they were killing the guard, Junior tried to make a run for it down the long hallway, but he was very slow in comparison to the athletic convicts that were after him.

As soon as they caught up to him, he was stabbed in his upper chest, near his right collarbone and again in his left leg, near the back of his knee. Then they were there in full-force20 armed officers unleashing relentless, violent blows with their batons on the remaining convicts that were still standing or still armed. Once the situation was contained and the injured transported to nearby emergency rooms at outside hospitals, it was declared that two of the four attackers were killed during the assault, and one federal corrections officer was also deceased. They ended up transferring Junior to another institution via Protective Custody, and it was here that he had gotten settled in while his attorney worked wonders on his appeal.

Apparently, there was a tremendous loophole in his case and he was wrongfully convicted, due to a violation of his constitutional rights, but for now he would have to sit and let his lawyer earn his fucking money!

He had formed alliances with some mobsters from Florida and also the Upstate New York areas, and he had promised them allegiance loyalty and he assured them that he would include their families in his takeover of the East Coast faction of the mafia.

All Junior did all day while he lifted weights and did his jumping jacks, was think about the reasons he was in this situation and the people he would personally pay back for their part in this predicament.That black cop bitch, Patricia. She would surely suffer tremendously for this shit! The daughter of his families' top hitman, Silvia Calzonetti who was his girlfriend at the time of his incarceration, had disappeared from the scene after he was arrested, and her infamous father Salvatore Calzonetti was dead; tortured and dismembered for his insubordination and betrayal.

Now, the only one left to pay back was the only son that Salvatore had, Tito Calversero, who was raised in Florida and earned his stripes as a young gangster down there until he eventually built up his own organization in the Miami areas. Surely he would die a terrible death at the hands of Joseph Canelli Jr. as soon as he was released from the Feds.

He was relaxing on his twin-size mattress when they called his name for a lawyer consultation visit.

"Canelli! Got an attorney conference buddy, get up!" said the corrections officer at the door to Junior's cell.

"It's about fucking time," was the reply that came from Junior, as he quickly sprung up from his bunk and got dressed.

His lawyer, a stout, chubby Jewish fellow named Fredrick Weiss, and he just so happened to be one of the most successful trial attorneys in the Essex County area, that dealt with mobsters. He carried only a manila envelope that was about ten by twelve and the type that only contained legal paperwork. He only toted a briefcase in the courtrooms he triumphed in.

"Mr. Weiss, what a pleasant surprise, how are you Sir?" Junior greeted his esquire in the presence of the corrections officer, smiling and shaking his clammy right hand. As soon as the officer left them alone in their segregated conference room, the real Joseph Canelli Jr. quickly rose to the surface,

"Listen here Freddy, you better have some fucking good fucking news for me, you know what I'm saying? I am sick and fucking tired of sitting around day in and day out in this fucking hellhole Freddy. You better have some good news is all I'm saying. Paying you a lot of fucking doe cheese here buddy," Junior verbally exploded, addressing his surprised lawyer.

"Here you go. This is for you Joey," said Mr. Weiss, handing Junior the huge envelope, while avoiding eye contact with the young deadly mobster.

After Joey Junior read the contents of the envelope in its entirety, he quickly read them to himself again and then he did something that he hadn't been able to do in some years now. He smiled.

"Does this mean what I think it means counselor? Am I really getting out of here ASAP?" Junior asked the attorney.

"Yes, that is exactly what it means Joseph. You are a free man, there is a change of clothes in the next room waiting for you and a limo outside to take you to the airport, congratulations," Fredrick Weiss said to his client.

As he flew home in a private jet, he bragged on the phone to his most recent girlfriend of six months, Sheila Falconia, another model turned mistress, turned Junior's possession for life. She had no idea what she was getting herself into.

"How were you released from jail so quickly baby?" Sheila asked him innocently and excited.

"It's like I told you doll face, they never had anything on me, and I don't know where the hell all of that "evidence came from but they had no fucking right in the first place to assault me, or violate my constitutional fucking rights as a human fucking being in this free world that we so happily live in, but searching my personal property which is the 4th Amendment of the Constitution," he boasted this to her while he had her on the speaker intercom.

"Really? Wow, that is so great Joey I can't wait to put these pretty lips on you and put you right to sleep after a great night tonight!" she excitedly exclaimed.

"Toots I had been jerking my dick for the last two years in the joint, I think I can wait one more day for a piece of ass. I got pressing business that will not wait, do you understand that?" he scolded.

"Yeah, I get what you are saying. See you tomorrow sweetheart. Have a safe flight home," she concluded.

"I will, love you too babe." He ended the call.

When Joey Jr. landed at Newark International, he was officially relieved to be home in New Jersey. He was greeted by ten of his goons and two underbosses (one of the underbosses was from the neighboring Comello Crime Family from out of the Kearny, Hoboken, Harrison, and Jersey City areas and Don Francisco Comello controlled those areas alone). It was not only a gesture of good faith and a show of support for Joey Junior, it was to show that they had nothing to do with the death of Don Vito Canelli, and that they were open for discussion in regards to some sort of business unification. Truth was that the old Don did not want a war with the Canelli Crime Family because he knew how ruthless and reckless young Joey Jr. was. His reputation preceded him. He would no doubt have the young future Don of the Canelli Crime Family killed should he refuse to unite and share territories as a form of truce. They would operate in parts of Essex County that the Canelli Crime Family controlled, and in return Don Comello would allow the Canelli Crime Family to set up operations in their controlled territories.

Before he saw his mother, before he saw his woman and had sexual relations, and before he even had a good home-cooked meal, Junior was business as usual and the very first order of business was to dethrone the acting boss of the family, Vincenzo Venettillo, who was the top capo at the time when Frankie, the underboss of the Canelli Crime Family was murdered. He was promoted by the Don himself when they had blew up Frankie's home, and the Don kept Vincenzo close to him as he groomed him as his underboss. Joey Jr. never liked Vincenzo. They were around the same age but while he was in prison, this motherfucker received my right due. Joey thought to himself often while he was out on his one-hour recreational period. Now, he would have to step down immediately as Don and assume a position once again as "capo" if he wanted to remain in the Canelli Crime Family.

Otherwise it would be war inside of the Canelli stronghold, and many lives lost. Joey Jr. had his own candidate for his new underboss, his longtime dear friend Romano "Rock" Lupo, whom had been there for Joey Jr. through good and the bad things they went through.

The meeting between the two families was set up at an Italian restaurant located in neutral territory in Irvington, called Lomberto's Villa. When all parties had entered and counted, it was clear that the acting Don of the Canelli Crime Family was not present. He was allegedly out of the states on other important family business back home. Young Joey Jr. took this as a sign of outright disrespect because he was the one that organized the sit down. Plus he was going to deal with the pending business within his own Canelli Crime Family, once Don Comello and his cohorts left, but coward-ass Vincenzo didn't show up. His plans would be temporarily delayed. Joey Jr. took the place of the acting Don for the Canelli Crime Family, and Don Comello took his place at the other end of the table, representing the Comello Crime Family. The Don spoke first.

"I am pleased that we could all come together and sit down peacefully Joey, and that we all could be here for your homecoming from prison. Welcome home! Salute!" voiced Don Comello, everyone at the table from both families following his lead as they all chimed in.

"Welcome home Joey! Salute!" they said in unison. Joey Jr. simply stood and raised his glass of vino in appreciation, then sat back down.

Don Comello took close notice to this "no words" gesture, and he did not like it.

"Let's get down to the business at hand shall we," Don Comello voiced to the table, and particularly to Joey Canelli Jr.

"Yes, let's get down to business gentlemen shall we," Joey Jr. stated, the words "shall we" being a code word that activated the soup-sipper sitting at the bar near the front door. He got the signal from the janitor who was mopping the floor two tables away from where the meeting was taking place. Once the janitor heard the words "shall we," he immediately went to the bar and ordered a "white Russian" and that was the code to alert the bartender to tell the guy at the end of the bar to leave the establishment. Approximately seven minutes after the guy left the restaurant, Joey Jr. excused himself to use the bathroom, and while he was in the bathroom, four armed robbers entered the restaurant with murderous intentions and they were not there to commit a mere robbery either, they were on contract.

"Everybody!" Boom! "Put your motherfucking hands where my eyes can see them! Get 'em up high and keep 'em there!" Barked the leader of the masked crew of armed robbers, letting off a single shot from the massive shotgun he held firmly with both hands, as the other three gun-toting shooters rushed toward the rear of the restaurant where the Italians were having their sit down.

"Everybody! Wallets and jewelry and hurry the fuck up!" yelled one of the shooters that was rushing towards the back with an open black pillow case. The others shooters carrying black pillow cases also, as well as shotguns. He didn't expect to see three Italian goons standing up with mini-Uzi's spraying bullets in his direction. Seven bullets tore into his face, chest, and shoulders as he dropped in front of his comrades. They immediately stared busting off shots from their shotguns, killing the three Italian mobsters and wounding several other mobsters that were in the immediate area.

While all of the shooting and commotion was going on, Don Comello was under the table hiding, and wondering where the hell Joey Canelli Jr. was, and how convenient it was for him to excuse himself right before the criminals burst in to rob the joint and then he saw them. He saw Joey Canelli Jr.'s shoes approaching the table. He remembered his shoes upon the initial introductions because were black and white wingtips the kind that they wore in the old gangster days and in the gangster films. Then, Don Comello heard the sound of a shotgun being chambered, and just seconds later, he saw the big weapon come underneath the table near his face. Then the incredible impact of the blast, deafening. Then, he was no more.

Joey Jr. had orchestrated the entire hit of course, and when he went into the bathroom all he had to do was go into the last stall, retrieve the red baseball cap and the automatic loaded shotgun, and put on the vinyl butchers apron over his suit. The red baseball cap was to show his hired team who he was and a clear signal not to shoot in his direction, he was the new boss.

Once he had blown Don Comello's head off, he immediately made sure that anyone who came along with the rival Don to the meeting was also dead. He turned his shotgun on the same underboss of the

Comello Crime Family who had accompanied the welcoming committee that greeted young Joey Jr. the very night he got out of prison, and with one swift motion he blasted off two rounds; one shot tearing into the right shoulder and the other, blowing off half of his face from the forehead back.

Only a raggedy bottom row of teeth remained of his face when he hit the floor dead. Joey Jr. quickly rounded up his crew from the melee, and they made their way out of the rear entrance to the restaurant without incident while they hired contractors stood behind and finished robbing the establishment and all of the patrons inside.

When word got out that Don Comello was murdered, along with his underboss Carmine Polletto from out of Jersey City, it was inevitable that a street war would follow immediately, and that the neighborhood morgues would be filled for weeks to come. Vincenzo Venettillo was infuriated. He could not control his anger when he addressed the situation following his business trip to the old country. He expressed his distaste for the ambush tactics that Joey Jr. used, and how he misled Don Comello to believe they were actually having a sit-down to discuss future business ties and an alliance against other mob families coming out of New York, Chicago, and Southern New Jersey, that were looking to get a piece of their territories.

An internal sit-down was called within the Canelli Crime Family, and this issue between Vincenzo and Joey Jr. would be solved once and for all. They were going to do it at one of the families' main clubhouses, The End Zone, a socialite club that dubbed as their headquarters and one of their personal spaces to relax and unwind with mistresses and such. It was also in the back room where some of the most secret of secrets were discussed and kept amongst the family.

Omerta was the code silence for life and sworn to never discuss the family business with anyone outside of the room where the discussion took place, not even with wives and children. Vincenzo insisted on the meeting to take place during the day-time because he did not trust young ambitious Joey Canelli Jr., even though it was being held at the very clubhouse that he had under his control. Still, the family name was Canelli and that was something that young Joey thought was his birthright automatically. He didn't take into account that sometimes families place people at the realm because they feel that they are the best fit person for that position at that moment in time for that particular family.

It was nothing personal, but his grandfather, Don Canelli, personally appointed Vincenzo to that seat and he was prepared to defend his views on the matter and move on as head of the family. Joey Jr. on the other hand, had no intentions of walking out of the meeting with the same title and rank he had when he walked in. He was coming out as the "new Don," the chief, the leader of the Canelli Crime Family. He had a surprise for old boy Vincenzo and Joey Jr. knew that he wouldn't even see it coming.

Joey Jr. arrived with Rock Lupo and six other goons twenty minutes after Vincenzo and his acting underboss, Alphonse Capetti, who hailed from the streets of Bloomfield all of his life. They had already arrived and searched the place from top to bottom, had it swept, etc... The acting boss and underboss were flanked by four gun-toting goons that were eager to prove themselves and step up in rank during this internal struggle for power. There would clearly be some promotions, as well as a lot of people getting clipped. Everyone from Vincenzo's entourage was very tense and on edge, and they were ready for action, ready to retaliate swiftly if some bullshit had jumped off at the meeting. Young Joey Jr. had a different approach altogether. He was way too smart and, he was more keen than people gave him credit for. Joey Jr. spoke first.

"Thank you all for coming to this very important meeting, as it directly or indirectly concerns everyone in this room. We are all here as a part of the Canelli Crime Family, my families' namesake, and we are here to clarify a few unclear points, and address certain subjects involving this family. Everyone seems to think that I am bloodthirsty for the seat of power in this family, but the reality is that this is my families' namesake so it doesn't matter who is the head of the family, I will still be and always remain Joseph Canelli Jr.!

No one can deny me that, or control what I do in the Canelli Crime Family. My great-grand father started this family with his two homeboys from the hood, and I grew up watching this family grow. Still, it is not my wish to disrupt or dishonor the wishes of my grandfather, the late Don Canelli. I will wait for my proper time to take the reins to this family when that opportunity is offered to me," he concluded. A surprised Vincenzo spoke up immediately in response to what seemed to be a sincere disclosure coming from Joey Jr.

"Well, I must say that I am sure I speak for everyone in this room when I say that I am very surprised and also pleased to hear these words come from you Joey Jr. Big Joey your father would be proud of you to make such a mature decision. It is for the best that we resolve these issues without incident or disrespect of any kind, it's better for the future of the family. We are all held accountable for our actions because we are held in the highest esteem as men of honor, men of our word, men of respect. We don't need any unnecessary turbulence interrupting the harmony we have established for many years already. I promised your father that I would seek his counsel on this matter and when I consulted him, he said it would be best to keep things as your grandfather, the Don has saw fit," Vincenzo said. What he concluded with, what he said lastly, pissed Joey Jr. off tremendously, but he suppressed his anger and just smiled at the table abroad. His time was coming. Then the acting underboss, Alphonse Capetti, tried to make like of the matter with a very bad, very wrongly placed joke.

"Yeah Joey. We thought we were all going shopping for bullet-proof vest and had to relocate our families. You know, just in case," he said, and then he smiled at an attempt to humor Joey Jr., which did not work.

"Well that just goes to show that you guys don't know me like I thought you knew me, not my style at all," he said, then smiled abroad and added, "Now please, let us lighten the mood in here and be merry, champagne please and red wine for everyone. It's a celebration for the Canelli Crime Family, I'm a fucking free man!" he concluded, raising his glass of wine.

"Cheers, to Joey Canelli Jr., and cheers to a long life of crime with this family," chimed in the acting Don Vincenzo Venettillo, as he too raised his glass and drank his toast. Every one of his soldiers followed his lead and did the same.

"Cheers!" they shouted together as they drank their champagne or wine.

Then Joey Jr., his best friend Rock Lupo, and all their goons all slowly sipped from their glasses and watched over the rims as the opposition slowly reacted to the poison that had laced the gold rims of their goblets, and chalices. It was a very powerful poison, both odorless and tasteless and just two drops could kill a fully grown horse or rhino. They all began to clutch at their throats as their glasses left their grasps, shattering on the table or hardwood floor, and they stared stunned and wide-eyed at their fellow mafia family members across the table. Unable to speak or yell out for help. The poison acted quickly, constricting their airways and cutting off their oxygen, and they collapsed writhing in pain, staring up at the ceiling and a bunch of grinning faces.

After the slaughter, Joey Jr. boasted that his first act as boss of the Canelli Crime Family, was to have the social club, The End Zone, burned to the ground immediately and they did not even remove the bodies from the premises.

Once the deed was done, Joseph Canelli Jr. was "upped" along with his best friend Rock Lupo, who was now the underboss of the Canelli Crime Family, and they began their reign. Unleashing vengeful vendettas on any enemy that the family ever had, they ordered and carried out over fifty murders in a matter of three weeks. Bodies were dropping everywhere, and whole crews were getting clipped, as well as some entire immediate families. They were merciless and reckless, but they didn't care about any of that, just as long as the word got out that if you crossed the Canelli Crime Family, then you or you and your entire family was fucking dead! They were already ruthless now with this "new power" as boss and underboss of the Canelli Crime Family, they were terrors.

Now that he was finally on top, he would now seek out revenge for the death of his dear grandfather, and he would finally pay back the black female officer that had him put away. "Boy did she have it coming to her," he thought to himself. And lastly, he would punish the only surviving offspring of that traitor Salvatore Calzonetti!

Chapter 13
Next Phase

As time the past by and wounds healed, everyone was preparing for the wedding of Diablo and Pretty Boy's sister, Melissa. They changed their minds about the destination wedding because of the death of Shorty Slice and had the necessary funds returned to them for the advances they had given for such things as vehicle transportation, motel bookings (they had booked two floors at the hotel, so they could be comfortable), and deluxe accommodations for everyone that attended the wedding. They just decided to do it really big, right there at home in the North Newark section near Bloomfield, at one of the biggest cathedrals the wedding planner could find in that area. They planned to be married in Newark, New Jersey and then take a two-week honeymoon/vacation in South Beach, Florida. Afterwards, they would get back to their lives as husband and wife, mother and father to their children.

The wedding was truly an event! The theme was lavender and cream, with the men that were participating wearing cream tuxedoes with lavender ties and matching lavender alligator shoes, and the women wearing lavender dresses, with cream designer headbands or some kind of designer scarf worn into or covering their hairstyles, and they all wore matching cream alligator pumps by Jimmy Choo. Everyone from the 50/50 Crew was in attendance, and her other brother, Shorty Slice's spirit was definitely in the room watching over them all.

Every one of the bosses also had their ladies in attendance with them of course, looking absolutely stunning and dripping in diamonds of all shapes and colors and Pretty Boy gave his sister away in the absence of their incarcerated father. Although it was supposed to be a private affair, an invitation-only event, there were several beautiful ladies present that did not have invites, and they were not there as well-wishers either. They actually had murderous intentions.

As Precious, Turquoise, Onyx, and Topaz of the Diamond Dolls sat quietly and listened to the nuptials being exchanged, they constantly glared at the members of the 50/50 Crew, staring daggers into their backs and the backs of their heads. They wish that they could wire the cathedral with explosives and bring the entire structure down upon the heads of their enemies, but there were entirely too many innocent bystanders in attendance, especially children, so they just endured the ceremony and waited for the reception to start, so that they could get closer.

The 50/50 Crew rented out the entire top two floors of one of the most lavish hotels near the airport, as well as the Grand Ballroom located on the ground floor. Everybody was dressed down from the wedding, yet still dressed to impress the night. Shoes and boots were worn both men and women, that cost in the thousands and it seemed as though everyone had decided to wear all of their diamonds that night also.

Draped in the most expensive tailor-made suits money can buy, the 50/50 crew met and greeted the new bride and groom with congratulations and each of the bosses handed Melissa a congratulations card with a check inside for ten million dollars. That offering from Speechless, Gorilla, Pretty Boy, and Chinky started a long line of well-wishers that stood there giving cash gifts as well, over one hundred people! Once the line had formulated, her new brothers-in-law and her biological brother, Pretty Boy, excused themselves to go meet and greet guest then discuss business.

As the 50/50 Crew and their guests mingled, the Diamond Dolls were working their way towards the crowd of ladies that seem to be laughing and talking up a storm about the wedding and Melissa's future plans after the honeymoon.

When they got closer, they listened while Melissa talked and bragged about how good it felt to be married. She wondered why she hadn't seen her girls at the wedding ceremony or the reception. She didn't even receive a text message from any of them, and that was very unusual for Sabrina, Kristina, Michelle, and Cheri.

The girls had been regular customers at the hair salon for over four years, and they had received invites for all of the functions and galas associated with Melissa. She always included them and made sure that they were V.I.P. at all of her parties. Oblivious to Melissa, was the fact that each one of her missing guests had been separately followed home by one of the Diamond Dolls from the salon. Then they had been killed and thrown in the trunks of their cars after all of their belongings were stolen from their vehicles, including the special invitations that were described by Paco's people who worked there at the salon. The invites were customized cream-colored satin and lace, with lavender embroidery and had a beautiful picture of the couple on the back of the entire invitation. They was very nicely done. She continued to talk about their decision to have the wedding in the States and the honeymoon in South Beach, Florida because of the recent family loss she had suffered. She bragged about the hotel arrangements that her new husband Diablo and her big brother Pretty Boy had taken care of, and all of the perks in package came with.

"She was a very pretty new wife," thought Precious of the Diamond Dolls. It's too fucking bad that she and her bitch-ass husband were going to get a serious fucking surprise when their asses get to South Beach. "Shit was NOT sweet in South Beach," she continued to relish in her private thoughts with a grin on her face, planning in her head. Once they heard the whereabouts of the hotel and resort, the length of stay, and that they were pretty much going alone for their honeymoon, Onyx then dipped off separating herself from the gossiping women and placed a call to Paco, her crazy-ass boyfriend and leader of The Terribles. After hearing everything that Onyx had to say, he instructed his animal crew to be on point, and to get ready for revenge. It would be payback for the death of their boss and founder, Baby Hatchet.

Melissa continued to talk, drink, and laugh with her guests and she had absolutely no idea what damages she had done, what calamities would soon follow, and what wars would ensue those disasters.

Once the reception and everything was behind them, Melissa and her new husband Diablo left their children in the care of Diablo's grandparents and flew to Miami International to begin their once in a lifetime honeymoon, and it was going to be a well-deserved vacation for them both, or so they thought. They partied and danced the night away every night, and drove around in exotic/luxurious rental cars during the day as they did their shopping, spending some of their wedding gift money. What they weren't aware of, was the five thugs that constantly and silently tailed them everywhere they went from the time they had stepped off of the plane. The five members of The Terribles were very anxious to kill anyone walking, but they got super-excited whenever it was an enemy!

They drove in three different taxi cabs, so it was very hard to pick up or spot a tail and besides, being stalked by someone was the last thing on the newlywed couples' minds. Melissa and Diablo was having the best time of their lives in South Beach, Florida enjoying their honeymoon, and by the third day down there they had accumulated enough shopping bags to fill up half of a small bedroom. Melissa talked to her big brother everyday on the phone, as well as a few of her best girls, and she would tell them all what a great time she was having with shopping and cruising on yachts with her new husband. She talked to Pretty Boy every single day. He suggested it, even though she had a thorough dude for a husband no doubt about it, he still felt as though she should be in contact once a day so that he knew that she was safe because he knew what the darker side of the tourist attraction was like and the locals were vultures when it came to the come-up, as it was in Anywhere, USA. Pretty Boy was always overprotective of his little sister all of her life.

One night while they were out on the town visiting one of the clubs, they were drinking and dancing and having a great time, just being to themselves in their own world of love and bliss. Out of nowhere, they were pretty much crowded on the dance floor and smothered by a bunch of couples that were dancing just a little bit too close for comfort. Then Mohawk of The Terribles decided that they weren't going to wait until they left the club to get the couple. He wanted to start some shit right then and there on the fucking dance floor, so he backed up while dancing and bumped into Diablo really hard, stepping on his foot in the process as he danced with Peridot and watched her step back to do a quick solo dance performance. As Mohawk stepped backwards, clapping his hands together to Peridot's dance moves, he purposely bumped into Diablo and stepped on his right foot to provoke the up north gangster.

"Hey! What the fuck man? Watch that shit bro. You didn't even say excuse me my man!" exclaimed an angry Diablo, screwing his face up at the Mohawk-hairstyle clown who had just bumped into him, putting out an extended arm towards Mohawk's chest to give the two of them some distance.

"Man fuck you cuz, who the fuck do you think you're talking to homeboy. You not in Jersey or New York motherfucker, this is the motherfucking bottom bitch! Fuck you nigga!"Bbarked a furious Mohawk at Diablo, getting hype aware that his boys were in close proximity and ready to strike. Melissa clutched Diablo's bicep and whispered to him,

"No baby, let it go papa. They don't even know you. We are on our honeymoon baby, remember?" she pleaded with her husband.

"Bitch, shut the fuck up!" said Tattoo, who was standing on Diablo's left side with his girlfriend Amethyst, who was also a member of the Diamond Dolls. Before Tattoo could get out another word of disrespectful remarks towards Melissa, Diablo had backed-out his switchblade in one swift motion and stabbed Tattoo right in the middle of his neck twice, then once in the chest near his heart. He just blanked out and went into protect-mode, worried about his beautiful wife.

He swung the knife at all of the people around him that appeared to be a threat, and when his knife connected with Money Moe's left shoulder, that's when he was stunned by eleven hundred volts from Paco's stun gun and the room went black. Once The Terribles had subdued Diablo, Melissa was also zapped by the high voltage, and then they were both quickly rolled up in throw rugs, transported out of the back of the club, and into an awaiting unmarked van never to be heard from again.

When Melissa finally regained consciousness, she struggled with her eyes to focus on the scene in front of her, and when her optics finally came into view, what she saw would haunt her dreams forever, even in death. She saw the remains of her husbands' body being hacked to pieces; his legs, his arms, his torso, his hands and feet, and his head were all separated and all she could do was scream her lungs out behind the gag that was secured around her mouth with duct tape, her eyes very wide with fear, as she shook uncontrollably! The Terribles just talked shit to the mutilated corpse as they hacked his body into pieces with hatchets, machetes, and hacksaws.

The five of them, Paco, Devious, Mohawk, Devil and Menace were all dressed in thick plastic coveralls and butcher aprons, with yellow rubber gloves that covered their forearms and were taped down to securely stay in place. Money Moe had been rushed to the hospital's emergency ward, and Tattoo had died on the scene from the knife injuries he sustained on the dance floor of the club where Diablo and Melissa were snatched up. As Melissa watched in terror and shivered violently, her eyes tried to survey the room from the far left of Diablos' body and then to the far right and once her eyes reached near the far right, just past Diablo's corpse towards the corner of the room, that's when she saw her. A female was videotaping the entire ordeal, probably from the time that they had been kidnapped, and it had appeared to be one of the girls that were dancing very close to her and Diablo.

As Onyx filmed the hideous crime and got all of the gory details on camera to view, she turned her lens towards the now awakened female captive, the sister of her enemy, Pretty Boy, of the infamous 50/50 Crew. Once she saw that the prisoner was staring right at her and into the lens of the camcorder, she smiled at her in the dimly lit dungeon/cellar and simply replied,

"This is for my sisters and my aunts bitch. You can thank your big brother and his crew for your fate when you see him in hell motherfucker!" she hissed at Melissa. Then Melissa felt her hair being pulled, but not in a sexual manner. It was being pulled straight up towards the ceiling in a forceful manner. Then she heard the girls' voice again. "This is my man Paco bitch, and he will do anything for me!" That was all that Melissa heard as the shadow stepped in front of her. Then Paco swung the machete with full force at her exposed slender neck.

Back home in Newark, New Jersey, Pretty Boy could not think straight and his heart had a pain that just would not go away, and it did not sit well with him. He was from the streets and he knew to always trust his instincts, and his instincts were telling him that something was terribly wrong with his sister down in Miami because it had been three whole days that went by without him talking to his baby sister, and she would NEVER ignore him and not check-in with him. She knew how much he would be worried about her.

SWITCH HITTER 2: 50/50 Crew: 'Til Death Do Us

He had contacted her hotel resort for any information on her and Diablo, but was only told by the management that they had checked out three nights ago, and had completely cleaned out their room when they left. Pretty Boy insisted that they check the surveillance videos of the hotel video cameras, and they told him that they would need a request from the police department to do that after a formal report for missing person would be filed and an official investigation started. After a few minutes of yelling into the telephone at the idiots on the other end, Pretty Boy assured them that he would be visiting them at the hotel soon, and he prayed that they would treat him the same way when they saw him in person.

His brothers and partners in the 50/50 Crew were there with moral support, and assured Pretty Boy that there had to be another explanation for Melissa and Diablo not being in contact with anyone back home. Like maybe a surprise extended honeymoon or something. Pretty Boy listened to his team, but he knew that that was some bullshit! He knew that something wasn't right.

Meanwhile, life went on at the beauty salon that Melissa owned, and the women who worked for her kept up their spirits, despite the fact that they were worried sick about their friend and boss. They all prayed everyday as a collective for her eventual return and safety, and that Diablo was fine as well; that all this worrying was for nothing.

It had been fourteen days since Melissa had been missing past her scheduled date to return home, and the ladies were all watching one of the popular morning shows on television when the mailman came in with the days' mail: bills, letters, magazines, and a large legal manila envelope. When the salon manager shuffled through the mail and came across the manila envelope, she paused and was apprehensive when she saw the bold words written across the envelope, in no particular handwriting: husband and wife. A tingle went through the lady as she held the package, turned it over and saw that in was postmarked Miami, Florida. Without even being conscious of it, she dropped the package and Juanita, one of the hair stylists came over and picked it up. Once Juanita read what was on the package, she ripped it open saying,

"Oh hell no! NO!" She opened package and took out the tape then quickly fumbled to put it in the DVD/VHS player, then pressed play.

The entire salon sat patiently waiting and watching, as some group of guys unloaded two rugs out of the back of some van and carried them into the side entrance of some warehouse. What they saw next gripped them with fear, as the unconscious bodies of Diablo and their dear friend Melissa were unrolled out of each rug.

"NO!" yelled Juanita, as Loretta the salon manager passed out and hit the floor. As women rushed to her aid, they were interrupted and frozen in their tracks by the loud screams of Diablo coming from the video. They all turned in horror and tried to watch the mutilation of Diablo, but once a customer had thrown up and another passed out from the gory scene, they decided to stop the tape and call her brother Pretty Boy immediately.

As soon as Pretty Boy got off the phone with Juanita, he called his crew individually and told them all to meet him at Melissa's beauty salon, and that it was an emergency! Speechless and Chinky had both gotten there before Pretty Boy because they were a little closer than he was to the location, and Jamaica who was driving Gorilla pulled up before Pretty Boy could get out of his car.

"They got a fucking tape of my sister and her husband man!" exclaimed Pretty Boy when they were all standing on concrete.

"What? What kind of motherfucking tape bro? What are you talking about?" asked Speechless as they were walking into the salon one by one.

When they were all inside, they could see right away that Juanita was pointing a shaky finger towards the television monitor on the wall, and they could also see that everyone inside of the salon was crying and had sad looks on their faces. Pretty Boy picked up the remote with a scowl on his face and pressed play because Juanita had told him she had rewound what they had already saw so far.

None of them were prepared for what was on the video, and despite the gasps and screams from the women in the salon, Pretty Boy just let it play as the tears ran down his face and he clinched his fists in anger. His 50/50 Crew, as well as everybody else in the hair salon had tears in their eyes and anger in their hearts. After Diablo finally stopped screaming because was either dead or he had passed out from the shock of being butchered, most of the women in the salon could no longer watch anymore of it. Some were crying uncontrollably, and others just could not stop vomiting. Then, those who could, watched in horror as the camera was slowly focused on Melissa, who was gagged with duct tape and bound tightly to a chair of some sort, and she was crying heavily. They all could hear the voice of the person holding the camera. It was a woman! She began explaining to Melissa why she and her husband were being murdered, and she didn't hesitate to reveal who was responsible for the couples' mutilation. They would all remember the name Paco and they all would NEVER forget the face of the female because after he chopped off Melissa's head and she filmed the head rolling on the floor, the bitch turned the camera towards her own self and whispered into the lens.

"We are coming for you 50/50 Crew. This is just the beginning motherfuckers, you just wait! You just wait!" she said with deadly intent.

"Oh my God! She was at the wedding and the reception," screamed Juanita. "I was wondering who she was the whole time there because she was always with three other females that looked like her, and none of them were socializing with everyone else! Oh my God Melissa!" She continued to scream and repeat, "Oh my God! Oh my God!"

Pretty Boy dropped to his knees in front of the television, clasped his hands together in prayer, and with waterfalls of tears pouring down his face, and right there he promised his baby sister and her husband Diablo, that their deaths would not go without retribution, and that everyone responsible for this, plus their families would die behind this violation or Pretty Boy would die trying to kill them all!

Everyone in the room bowed their heads in unison with him.

They were gangsters so of course involving the police was out of the question! This was more personal than anything that had hit home with the 50/50 Crew. It was just as heavy as when Chinky was in Miami dying after the massacre at Ballers and Broads strip club, and just as serious as when Shorty Slice was murdered by the Nigerians, except it was Melissa, Pretty Boy's baby sister, who was just like a sister to them all, and she was an innocent! They would spare no one when the 50/50 Crew went after their enemies in Miami. Not one soul.

Chapter 14
Red River

Following the murders of his sister and her husband Diablo, after they secured things in their organization with their most trusted captains and lieutenants in New Jersey, Pretty Boy and his 50/50 Crew partners took to the streets of Miami, Florida with no mercy or leniency. Whoever had a problem with them asking questions in the area, would regret it immediately! They were in Florida three days after the viewing of the video.

They started at the hotel, and with the manager in charge of running the place, the very same manager that gave Pretty Boy the runaround before they were sent the tape of Melissa's kidnapping and murder. His name was Richard Hernandez, and he was a fake-ass playboy/supervisor who flirted with every married or non-married woman in the immediate area, employee or guest, it didn't matter to him. Pretty Boy approached him with malicious intentions.

"Hey man, are you the guy in charge around here? Hey! Motherfucker! I am talking to you Richard! Are you in charge around here?" Pretty Boy demanded, but he already knew the answer to that, he just wanted to catch the guy of guard, as he did.

"Excuse me, uh yeah man. I am Richard, the hotel manager here at our lovely resort. What can I do for you? How may I be of assistance?" the nervous hotel manager asked Pretty Boy, as he eyed the small menacing entourage that was with his questioner.

"How may you help me? You can show me to your office motherfucker!" ordered Pretty Boy, and with that he signaled to Gorilla, who grabbed up the hotel manager and strongly escorted him to the office he directed the 50/50 Crew towards.

"Hey, wait a minute. What's going on? What's the mean-" he started, but his words were cut short by Gorilla's gigantic hand covering his mouth and chin.

"Shut the fuck up or you die in the next hour bitch. This is a motherfucking business call. That means that we mean motherfucking business hoe and that there is nothing social about this visit bitch, do you understand that?" barked Speechless, giving anyone that was paying attention to what was going on the deadliest of looks, basically telling them to mind their motherfucking business, including the security.

They all forced their way into the nearby office while Chinky stood at the door outside armed to the teeth with four weapons that couldn't be seen by just looking at him.

As soon as they got him inside of his office, the 50/50 Crew put on the video and made him watch it. Just the end when they had decapitated Melissa.

"That was my motherfucking baby sister you just watched die pussy-ass-smart-mouth motherfucker, and I am the same one that called up here to this resort asking about her weeks ago when she disappeared!" barked Pretty Boy into the terrified hotel manager's face. "It was you that gave me the runaround motherfucker, and it was you who acted like an asshole when I wanted some information about my sister and the surveillance tapes from the hotel security cameras pussy! Now you are going to help me as much as you fucking can bitch!" Pretty Boy grimaced as the words hissed out of his mouth.

"We need the security tapes for last month and from this month as well and we need them like yesterday motherfucker so hurry the fuck up, and make sure that we have all of the surveillance of this entire place!" ordered Speechless.

"Okay, okay. Give me just a second. Oh my God! I'm so sorry! I'm so sorry you guys," said the shaking hotel manager, as he reached for all of the video evidence the 50/50 Crew demanded. Then on their way out of the door, once they had got all the evidence that they had come for, Pretty Boy hauled off and punched the nervous hotel manager in his face so hard, that he shit his pants when he hit the floor.

"If I find out that you were involved in any way, then your whole family is dead bitch!" Pretty Boy told the unconscious big mouth hotel manager.

After they left the hotel, they all headed over to Tito's mansion in Miami to look at every single piece of footage the hotel/resort had acquired since Melissa and Diablo's arrival. Tito and Pretty Boy had never formally met, even though Tito had made an appearance with his two personal goons at Shorty Slice's entombment service. He didn't stay for any introductions. Only to pay his respects to Speechless, his half-brother, and his family. Now, they were able to meet and talk face-to-face under similar circumstances, but different, Tito had a sister too.

"Nice to finally meet you Tito. As I understand it, you are family and I would like to express my gratitude for granting us access to your place and your equipment, and for what you did for my brother Chinky down here," Pretty Boy said as he shook Tito's hand then embraced him in a hug.

"Likewise, Pretty Boy. I am sorry for your loss my brother, and as far as my house goes, my castle is your castle," Tito expressed, waving his hand across the front of his body to emphasize what he was saying.

"Thank you Tito. Now I hear that you have some state-of-the-art satellite shit up in here, and we really need to get these motherfuckers something serious!" Pretty Boy said, becoming angered.

"Say no more," replied Tito, gesturing towards a room that was full of equipment: screens, monitors, microphones, etc... Both of his goons were experts in surveillance as well because they went to a local school for audio and technological training before they were handpicked by Tito to join his fold. Now Tony and Marko wore several hats and had numerous positions.

"Marko, please assist Pretty Boy and his crew with all the help they need, and take your time this time," Tito said.

"No problem Tito, anything you guys need I am your man. Let's track down these dumb motherfuckers shall we!" replied Marko. Then he took the discs from the resort that Pretty Boy handed him and went to work.

Tito had to take care of some very important business up in New Jersey regarding Joey Canelli Jr., because he had gotten news a while ago about his possible return home to New Jersey, and now it was confirmed along with the new wave of violence between the families up there. Now it was time for him to answer for what he did to Tito's sister!

Tito left for the private jet immediately after making sure that that 50/50 Crew was good with everything that they needed for the time being, taking Tony with him and five other goons that were under Marko and Tony, but were just as skilled and vicious. They were only younger and lower in rank.

It didn't take Marko long before he did his magic and pieced together right before the 50/50 Crew's very eyes, some of the people involved with Melissa and Diablo's abduction and eventual murder. It showed the same group of individuals pulling in and out of the parking lot of the resort and also in the lobby, elevators, and hallway where the couple honeymooned because apparently they came back to clean out the room of all traces of their captives. The time on the video revealed that it was only 2:15 a.m. when the eight goons and two females entered the suite two-by-two five different times. Then again at 3:10 a.m., the video footage showed them leaving with many shopping bags and garbage bags, all at the same time from the room. The video also revealed something else to Pretty Boy and the 50/50 Crew that the hotel/resort manager, Richard Hernandez was directly involved.

Tito and his entourage arrived at Newark International Airport without any incidences, and they were ready for the task at hand tracking down Joseph Canelli Jr. and bringing him to Tito alive or at least a picture of him dead with a bullet in his motherfucking head! That was their briefing. Nothing left to be said except kill any motherfucker that is non-compliant!

They all ate a big, hearty breakfast before they set on their quest for the whereabouts of Joey Canelli Jr., and after all the steaks and eggs, and pasta and Italian sausages, they each drank a glass of orange juice. The seven of them drove in two separate rentals. A green Dodge Caliber and a maroon Dodge Charger, with Tito, Tony, and two soldiers, Johnny and Tim riding in the Caliber and Ronnie, Jimmy, and Joey Knife riding in the Charger.

Each of the cars they were riding in smoothly searched the streets of Bloomfield, Caldwell, Montclair, Bellevue, and North Newark as though they owned the streets. They were extremely confident, and supremely armed with the best semi-automatic and fully-automatic weapons that money can buy, and they were playing for keeps. His sister, Sylvia Calzonetti, had been missing since she had gotten Joey Jr. arrested, and it was presumed in the mafia world, that she was long dead. She still had not received her share of her inheritance of ten million dollars from her slain father, Salvatore Calzonetti, who was the chief assassin for many years with the Canelli Crime Family. Salvatore had left behind three things that were securely kept away from everyone in the world, except his son Tito Calversero: twenty-one million dollars for his son and daughter to receive ten million dollars and eleven million, a detailed list of instructions for Tito to carry out, and his journal to which Speechless would be the recipient of. Tito had not planned on giving the journal to Speechless until he found his sister, or at least got answers for her disappearance. He just wanted closure. Once he got that, he would carry out the commands of his fathers' will.

It wasn't until they all were riding through West Orange, that they finally spotted one of the clubs that were on the list of possible whereabouts for Joey Canelli Jr. A small, yet lavish pool hall/bistro that doubled as one of the meeting places for the Canelli Crime Family according to Little Gus, who was still with the Canelli Crime Family, but had undeniable loyalty to Salvatore Calzonetti. Some years ago, Salvatore Calzonetti was ordered to kill Little Gus' father and uncle, who were both capos in a rival family's crew that were threatening to get stronger and impeded the future plans of the Canelli Crime Family. Gus was just a teenager, when Salvatore entered their home with deadly intentions and spotted the youngster. He hesitated and then he left the home without harming anyone. Still, he told the two brothers that they had to leave the East Coast, and that they were never to return again. They were allowed to let young Gus stay and be raised in New Jersey by his mother and grandmother, but when he got older and became a gangster, he joined the Canelli Crime Family and was a very loyal soldier. He never forgot what Salvatore had done for him, and he knew that he, his father, and his uncle were all dead that day the killer had entered their home. Now, here he was, providing information to Tito that could no doubt cost him his life, but he didn't care. He felt it was very wrong the way that the Canelli Crime family did Salvatore.

They pulled into the small parking lot of Anna's Billiards and Bistro one by one and parked next to two black limos that had jet-black tinted windows, so Tito and his crew knew that the cars belonged to mafia figures. Either that, or some kind of fucking diplomat was visiting Anna's, and that shit wasn't likely. They didn't waste any time because this was not a fucking ordinary visit. This was punishment for Joey Canelli Jr. putting his hands on Tito's sister and threatening her life, and that sanction was death, point blank period. Once Tito got the answers to his questions about Sylvia's whereabouts, then Joey Jr. was dead. Either way, answers or no answers, he was a fucking dead man! They screwed the silencers unto their automatic pistols and entered the social club with guns at their sides.

"I am I friend of the Canelli Family. Where can I find little Joey Jr.?" asked Tito to the female bartender, keeping his eyes locked with hers.

"I'm sorry, who did you say you were?" she asked as she looked towards the back room and attempting to hit the alarm to warn the mobsters in the back.

Tito lifted his silenced Beretta and shot her in the forehead.

"I didn't," he said, as her body dropped and his goons sprang into action shooting anyone who looked as though they were going to interfere as they all worked their way to the back room where you could smell cigar smoke, hear loud talking and cards shuffling behind the door.

"Nobody survives you guys, hear me? Nobody!" ordered Tito, as they got closer and closer to the door, every gun drawn.

"Knock this motherfucker down Joey Knife!" ordered Tito, signaling to Joey Knife, who was holding a one-man battering ram.

"Yeah boss," responded Joey Knife, lifting the battering ram and swinging it towards the upper hinge of the door. Then in one quick motion, he swung it towards the lower hinge knocking the door loose. Immediately the crew stormed inside, to a barrage of gunfire, shooting everyone within the dwelling, looking for Joey Jr. but he was nowhere around.

There were eight guys inside of the back room playing poker and talking shit about the recent takeovers and assassinations committed by the Canelli Crime Family, at Joey Juniors' request because he wanted it all! Even families that were close with the Canelli Crime Family, trusted them, and held them in the highest esteem, were crossed and shot dead one-by-one, day by day. They were caught slipping and murdered. They were all laughing and joking about this black crew that were all caught by surprise and killed by the Canelli family, who use to employ their services when they needed a rival mobster murdered outside of the neighborhood. The blacks had most of an entire city near North Newark on lockdown with heroin and cocaine, and the Canelli Crime Family wanted Kearny completely under their control, so the black hit-men had to be eliminated. While they were sitting there clowning around and talking about their victims, the door sounded with a deafening "BOOM" and before they could draw their weapons and shoot, another "BOOM" came from the bottom of the door. Then it was off and there were bullets flying towards them with no sound as they attempted to shoot back. "Silencers!" thought Bruno, who was in charge of the goons at the social club. He started to fire once he saw that the intruders were not the fucking cops or the Feds. One of Bruno's wild bullets struck Ronnie in the left eye as he rushed through the door squeezing off silenced shots and dropped him instantly. Then Bruno went down from shots fired by Tito and Johnny simultaneously into his chest and face. The rest of the guys from Tito's crew forced their way into the room overpowering the Canelli family goons and killed all of them, with no sight of Joey Jr. anywhere! Tito was furious! Not only because he didn't locate his target, but because he had lost a crew member in this first encounter in New Jersey, and now he had to kill at least ten of Joseph Canelli Jr.'s family members! It was on.

 Joey Canelli Jr., had gotten word hours later about the massacre at the social club in West Orange because there were no witnesses, so he had to wait to see it and hear it on the news. He could tell that this was a hit on his life, and the fact that there were no witnesses left alive to tell any kind of stories about what happened, confirmed his assumptions about the attempt on his life. He was furious, and he wanted immediate answers! After he went over it in his head time and time again, he decided that it could only be one of two possible enemies that could be after him with such vengeance. One, being the relatives of Don Comello seeking retaliation for his murder, and the other, the brother of that betraying bitch Sylvia, and son of that fucking traitor Salvatore Calzonetti! Coming to those conclusions, he immediately assembled a 20-man team in four different vans and began to comb the streets, hoping to run into his enemies before they ran into him! He went to every single spot that he was affiliated with or had control over and it was as though he and Tito had been just missing each other because where Tito and his crew visited and massacred mobsters at two other social clubs in their hunt for Joey Jr., he was two stops behind them with his own mob of Canelli Crime Family goons.

They were almost set to give up their search for the top mobster, and Tito had to get his wounded soldiers looked at and taken care of by emergency physicians, so they were heading towards Bayonne where Tito had ties through his father and they were professionals of the highest order. As Tito talked on the phone with his people in Florida to let them know he would be home soon and that his time away from them might not be as long as he thought it would be, he looked back from his passenger seat and checked over his soldiers again. He told the driver,

"Step on it Tony, we have to get them to the doctors'"!

As the two vehicles accelerated in unison and ran a red light that had just turned, suddenly the lead car Tito was riding in was caught off guard and cut off by a black van that had the sliding side door already open. It was too late for them to react. A fierce burst of automatic gunfire from a Vector hit the front of the car shattering the windshield, destroying the radiator, and flattening one of the two front tires. Bullets ripped through the hood of the Caliber as the driver Tony was hit in the face and half of his right cheek was blown-off along with his right ear lobe. He had glass in his face and in his eyes, but he didn't let that stop him from trying to maneuver the car and get them all to safety as he reached for his shoulder holster and started shooting his still silenced Beretta through the missing windshield back at their ambushers.

Tito, who was also grazed in the face by the high caliber bullet and hit in the left side of his chest twice, reached down to retrieve one of the mini-Uzis they brought with them and as the car swerved around the van, he aimed his weapon at the driver and fired repeatedly! The sound of rapid, repetitious gunfire ripping through the air and shattering glass temporarily caught Tito's attention as he witnessed the other vehicle, the Charger, carrying his soldiers being ripped apart by two gunners with TAR-21s shooting from another van. One shooter was laying on the floor of the van while he shot his weapon, and the other stood up right next to him shooting his TAR-21. Tito could do nothing. The gas tank was hit and he watched the other car burst into flames, as Joey Knife jumped out on fire and was repeatedly cut down in a hail of bullets as he fell to the pavement dead.

"Tony! Get us the fuck out of here now!" barked Tito, reloading and spraying his Uzi at the assailants again.

"Okay!" replied Tony. He then floored the vehicle as the other two enemy automobiles gave chase, shooting relentlessly at the fleeing Caliber.

"Turn here!" ordered Tito. "Take them down the alley and-" he started to tell Tony to lose them, but was hit from behind through the back windshield in his upper right shoulder. "Ah shit!" Tito yelled, as he absorbed the impact and felt the fire. "Grenades!" he yelled to the wounded goons in the backseat. Johnny and Tim, on cue, pulled the pins of the grenades they took from the backpacks in front of them on the floor at their feet, and tossed them out of their windows towards the pursuing vans. The grenades were on point and perfectly thrown, because the first one blew up just as it rolled towards the rear wheels of the first van, and then the second one exploded right at the beginning of the van, leaving the van disabled and its' passengers wounded badly, or dead. The immobilized van was just what they needed to escape the massacre because it denied the other advancing van a clear passage to continue the chase, allowing Tito and his crew to get away!

Inside the second van, Joey Canelli Jr. cursed aloud and showed his anger when he realized that they had no chance of catching the fleeing hit men but he was sure he would get another chance at them, and he would be ready!

He handed the loaded F2000 he was gripping tightly to one of his soldiers in the back of him and told him to put it away!

Now he <u>knew</u> who was responsible for the raids on his spots and the deaths of his soldiers because he had seen his face when the van he was in took out the burgundy Charger that the other hitters were in. He saw him through the front passenger window as he shot at the other van, and he remembered him from their initial introduction when he first started to date Sylvia. It was Salvatore Calzonetti's son,

SWITCH HITTER 2: 50/50 Crew: 'Til Death Do Us

Tito Calversero.

Once Tito and the remaining half of his crew made it out of harms' way, they weren't too far from Bayonne where the doctors were located, so they pressed on. Had they had any run-ins with the police or any other kind of law enforcement in route to their rendezvous in Bayonne, there would be hell to pay because Tito was NOT going to prison, ever! They slowed down their speed once they were maybe twenty miles from where the ambush had went down, and Tito realized he was losing a lot of blood, as was Tony, who seemed to be losing consciousness as he drove.

"Hold on Tony, we are almost there. Just a few more streets and traffic lights partner, hold on man, we are going to be alright!" comforted Tito, as he himself grimaced in pain.

"Can't do it boss. Been holding on since they rushed us back there man. Feel dizzy, light-head," uttered Tony before he passed out and crashed the vehicle they were in into a curb, then a tree.

"Tony! NO! Look out, watch out!" yelled Tito, as he braced for impact when he saw his comrade's forehead hit the steering wheel after he blanked-out. The Caliber crashed with a tremendous thud because Tony never hit the brake pedal when he crashed. Quickly, the remaining three got out of the car after Tito lifted Tony's head off the steering wheel to prevent the car horn from sounding off continuously, and took what they could conceal, grabbing two duffel bags out of the truck and loading what weapons they could carry in their condition. Tito was hurt bad, so he called Speechless to let him know what the deal was and that he had something very important to discuss with him as soon as possible!

"What the fuck bro? You just sit tight, and give me your location now! I will have a car pick y'all up immediately Tito!" stated Speechless.

"Ok," replied Tito, then he gave Speechless the name of the street they were on and the address they were standing in front of when he made the call. Then the three injured Italian mobsters started to walk.

As they walked down the long strip of street, continuously looking over their shoulders, proceeding with caution, an all-white Mercedes Benz S600 pulled up slightly in front of where they were walking because the driver was warned not pull up on them directly. They could see the front passenger window rolling down and then they saw a young black male stick his head out the window.

"Tito! Help is here for you guys, hurry and get in. We are family, Speechless sent us!" said Little Mike-Mike, who had been with the 50/50 Crew for three years loyally as a driver/shooter, and who had been instructed to treat Tito and his guys with the utmost respect. Little Scooter and Little Terrell (who was driving the Benz) hopped out to help the wounded gangsters into the car, and put their duffel bags quickly in the trunk. In an instant, they were speeding towards Bayonne and following Tito's specific instructions.

By the time they had reached the doctors' house/office, Tito had lost a substantial amount of blood and was losing all consciousness. The doctor and his assistant, along with Little Terrell and Little Scooter helped the severely injured gangsters into the office and to the necessary operating tables to begin preparations. Tito asked Little Terrell to call his boss, Speechless and to pass him the phone.

"Hello? What's up Lil' T.?" asked Speechless.

"It's me, Tito. Listen I'm hit up pretty bad. Some heavy heat they came with brother. In case I don't make this trip back you need to know two very important things. One, the motherfuckers responsible for my death, they are the Canelli Crime Family, Joseph Canelli Jr. to be specific. He must die if I don't survive, promise me bro! Listen, there's something my father left for you. Some sort of diary that he only wanted YOU to have. He made me promise that I would honor his will a very long time ago. That time has come. I know that you are busy down there, but you need to get up here ASAP because I lost a whole lot of-" he dropped the phone that Little Terrell had passed him, as Tito went under.

Speechless explained to his family in the 50/50 Crew that shit was extremely urgent with Tito back in New Jersey, and that he had to be out! He told them (which they already knew), that he would be back as soon as he could.

He took the jet and was in Newark in no time and then he had his driver pick him up and shoot him over to Bayonne where Tito and his boys were holding up.

When he pulled up to the house, Tito was almost dead. He was holding on for Speechless. He was holding on so that he could look into the eyes of the person he was going to entrust his families' future safety with. He needed to look into his eyes as he promised him he would live up to these expectations and carry out the request put before him.

"Tito, I am here bro. Are you awake?" asked Speechless, as he approached the bed Tito was in. There were wires and monitors everywhere around him.

"Come closer brother. Come closer to me. Dad made me promise to make you make... sure that you... got this diary that belonged... to... him," he struggled to say, as he reached under the sheet that was covering him and with half-closed eyes, passed Speechless the journal of Salvatore Calzonetti. Unbeknown to them both, the diary contained the most sensitive and personal memoirs of the notorious mob hit-man and many other things, that Speechless would soon find out as he read the journal in the days and nights to come. Things that would alter his life even more.

It was a thick, old condition on the outside (but later on Speechless would find out that it was very well-kept indeed on the inside), black and gold diary that had to be about 300 pages thick. He rubbed his thumbs across the front of the cover and then down the length of the gold-tipped pages of the journal, then he put it in his bag for safe keeping upon his return to Florida.

"Tito, talk to me brother and tell me what you can but try to reserve some of your strength, if that is even possible," Speechless asked the mortally wounded gangster, his adopted brother.

"This... motherfucker and his... whole family are the reason my pop is no longer with us. Motherfuckers killed him. They killed Sylvie too!" struggled Tito telling his half-brother what he must do.

"Where is he?" demanded Speechless.

"He is everywhere, can be anywhere. His town, his area. He is no dummy, we thought we had him," mumbled Tito, telling Speechless everything with his eyes half closed.

"Are you going to make it through this brother? Can you hold on and fight this? They are sending for more blood for you! I need you Fight this shit Tito! Be strong Bro! Don't let this take you out!" Speechless began to raise his voice in urgency, as he watched the life being drained from his half-brother as he lay in the hospital bed slipping away.

"You take care of yourself Speech. Hold your crew down and keep… your promise to me. I will tell Pop you said hello, okay?" he managed to get those important words out before he flat-lined.

"Tito! Don't do this shit man. There is much to get done my brother! Tito! Don't do this bro, we got a lot of things to take care of man!" Speechless expressed to the figure laying in the bed, but his words fell on deaf ears, as his half-brother Tito Calversero, the only biological son of his mentor and godfather, Salvatore Calzonetti, was dead.

By the time he had got there, the emergency doctor at the private hideaway residence out in Bayonne had informed him that Tito had suffered multiple gunshot wounds from a high-caliber assault rifle, and that one of the bullets had hit a main artery causing an extensive loss of blood. The doctor explained that there was no way a man could survive by losing the amount of blood that Tito had lost, and that surely the man had to be running on pure adrenaline or some sort of unknown inspiration because he had clearly lived that long after the assault. He also told Speechless that the amount of blood loss would surely kill Tito probably before the additional blood supply could get back to him in time.

The doctor and his assistants were able to save the young lives of Tito's soldiers Johnny and Tim, and although they would be forever scarred by the, the minor disfigurement was nothing in comparison to the lives of their comrades and their boss, that were lost in the ambush. They would go back to Florida and continue to soldier-up under the leadership of Marko, who would now be the boss in wake of Tito's sudden demise. Until they got back to Florida, they would follow the directions and instructions of Speechless, who they knew were very close to their deceased boss.

Speechless made arrangements for Tito's body to be transported to the Sunshine state with Tim and Johnny, and he got back to Florida as soon as he could after dealing with this tremendous loss. One thing was for certain though. He had every intention on avenging his half-brother, and unknown to Tito's knowledge, his father death had already been avenged when Don Vito Canelli was murdered in the bathroom of his own home!

SWITCH HITTER 2: 50/50 Crew: 'Til Death Do Us

Once he was back in Florida, he had to let his brothers in the 50/50 Crew know what time it was with Tito and the members of his crew that passed on as well. Marko took shit extremely hard and close to heart, because he was very close with his boss Tito, and his best friend of many, many years, Tony.

He would have a serious hand in dealing with the people that killed his friend and his boss. He would be on the front line to the very end of this journey to retribution. The 50/50 Crew updated Speechless on the recent developments with tracking down The Terribles, and told him that they were anxious to end this business in Florida and get back to New Jersey, because every day that Melissa and Diablo's killers lived was A day too long! They told him that they had taken the resort/hotel manager, and had interrogated him to the point where he confessed to giving his people the information about Melissa and Diablo's whereabouts. He told the Terribles exactly where to find the couple, and when they had left their room that fateful night to enjoy themselves on the town. Pretty Boy and the 50/50 Crew also found out, that the Diamond Dolls were the main ones responsible for the kidnapping and murders of Melissa and Diablo, and that they had recruited the services of their crazy love-sick counterparts to carry out the contract.

"So where the fuck are they at?" asked Speechless of his crew, looking everyone square in the eye one by one.

"We know where they are and where they live!" said Pretty Boy to Speechless. "We were waiting for you to get back brother. We found them!" Pretty Boy concluded, very eager and excited.

"Good! Outstanding! Now let's go sit the fuck down and talk about the layout. We got a lot of motherfuckers to kill down here, a whole lot of motherfuckers!" expressed Speechless, with one of the most intense stares on his face.

The 50/50 Crew rented out two beach houses in the same area they had vacationed in as an entire family a while ago, back when Uzi Malik and Shotgun Shawn were still alive and there was more than enough space for everyone present. Speechless and his team of bosses were ready to avenge Pretty Boy's baby sister and her husband, and anyone else that died as a result of this war. They had flew down an addition twenty shooters and had a few boxes of the latest heavy hardware shipped via private jet along with the hungry soldiers that would voluntarily give their lives in the cause of war for the 50/50 crew. Crates of MP5K's, Famas, Vectors, Bullet-proof vests, and F2000's were shipped with the goons and then transported by the limos that picked them up at the private airstrip, once they got to Miami. They were all put up in the beach house and not in any of the nearby hotels or motels, because Speechless wanted everybody on the team to be close and not to stray away from the unit or get caught slipping in any way. The guns were immediately unpackaged and distributed to everyone present and then they were given a vest, extra ammunition, plus a handgun and a grenade in case of any emergencies. They were then instructed to follow the leadership of the person placed in charge of their unit, and to kill any motherfucking enemy they came across! The orders were clear, and the mission was retribution!

They went over the plan, and drew up a diagram of all the known areas where The Terribles ruled or hung out on a daily basis. Then, they matched the individual members of The Terribles to the information they received from Richard the hotel/resort manager about their families and their family's addresses. Then after that, they matched up what Diamond Dolls they could with the members of The Terribles that they knew about and where they were located.

Chapter 15
Vindictive Retribution

The first order of business down in Miami was to create chaos and worry amongst The Terribles and The Diamond Dolls, by blowing up the houses of their relatives, and making sure that they were all dead and stinking! The 50/50 Crew would spare no one in their ultimate quest for revenge. They didn't care who you were. If you were inside of one of the residences, businesses, or safe houses on the list of addresses that was in the 50/50 Crew's possession, then you were just out of luck, because the shooters were coming through after the fire bombings and making sure that everyone in the place was dead! The bosses in the 50/50 Crew didn't want anyone to almost survive the onslaught. They wanted every person to die for the deaths of Melissa and Diablo, and they wouldn't settle for anything less than that! This was very close to home and this violation would not go unpunished. No matter what it took, or how long it took, they would surely get their retribution on these new enemies. When they tortured and questioned the hotel manager, he told them everything! From his involvement with The Terribles and how he "set up" tourist and visitors all the time from different states to get robbed, raped, or kidnapped and killed; he told them all that he knew. He gave up whereabouts and locations of hide-outs, he gave up addresses that he knew of, and he also gave up addresses of some of the Diamond Dolls he knew of or had visited.

As soon as the 50/50 Crew felt as though they had extracted enough information from this member of The Terribles crew, Gorilla took him on a short ride. He parked the rental and retrieved the hotel manager's bound and gagged body out of the trunk, sat him up against the wall of an alleyway right next to a huge dumpster, and shot him in the face with a .50 Caliber Desert Eagle four times until there was nothing but a bloody pulp atop his slumped shoulders.

Once Gorilla got back to the fold, he and his boss partners came up with the ultimate plan and it was time to put the plan into effect. They would go after the leaders of the crew called The Terribles, and all of the soldiers and sergeants would firebomb all of the homes and business of their families and relatives of The Terribles and the Diamond Dolls. It was clearly ordered that no one survive this massacre, and that those placed in charge of the hit teams make sure that no one was left alive. To insure this permanent extinction, they would set up two shooters armed with mini Uzis at the backs, fronts, sides of every home and business that was to be blown-up, so that if anyone managed to live through the explosions and tried to escape through any windows or others outlets in order to avoid the fires, they would surely be cut down.

The eight killers assigned to each spot, were to take up post before the grenades and the cocktails were even thrown because anyone outside before the bombs were tossed were getting shot and killed for sure! They were equipped with gasoline cocktails and fragment grenades, as well as the latest heavy hardware, and when they hit The Terribles, no one would see it coming; not that <u>soon</u>.

Meanwhile, as the bosses of the 50/50 Crew prepared to leave and carry out the necessary hits on the leaders of their enemies, as the armed rentals full of shooters and killers rolled out one by one, the six cars were packed to capacity with soldiers and artillery. Once the leaders gave the word, they rolled out in Luxury rentals. A black Ferrari Modena, which contained Speechless and Pretty Boy and a cherry-red Bentley GT coupe, which held Gorilla and Chinky. As soon as the young shooters saw their leaders leaving as the two luxury vehicles began to roll out in an opposite direction, they pulled off and proceeded to execute "Operation Elimination" as so it was called by Pretty Boy.

The 50/50 Crew leaders pulled up on one of the major strips where the bosses of The Terribles were known to be hanging out at and were the most comfortable because no one would ever dare to come near that territory to bring drama to The Terribles gang of crazy killers. When they pulled up to the curb, they could see the barrage of stares and grills from onlookers who were clearly workers and soldiers on the block they occupied. They seemed to be in awe of the cars, but at the same time they were cautious and apprehensive as to who were the occupants of theses expensive sports cars. Then the workers and shooters thought that, possibly it could be the plug and they were there to survey the area that they so heavy invested in on a monthly basis every year. With Gorilla and Chinky parked directly behind them, the drivers and passengers side windows of both cars began to roll down once they recognized three of the leaders from the pictures they studied and carried with them on this day of murderous attacks. It was Money Moe, Mohawk, and Paco! They all remembered Paco clearly from the video; the footage that would forever be embedded in their memories from the very first time they watched it. As the windows came down, the music came blaring from both cars luxury sports cars at the same time. It was the local radio station, and they were playing "Shut Up!" from one of the hottest artist and musical pioneers of the Miami hip hop music scene. The music momentarily disguised the sound of the massive automatic weapons being cocked, and before the ground troops could react to anything, the area was suddenly invaded by sounds reminiscent of a war movie! People tried to run and hide as the first tremendously loud shots went off, but then once they saw that their leaders were the first to be shot, most of them tried to retrieve weapons and fight to defend their turf against the intruders. Paco, Money Moe, and Mohawk all got mowed down along with three others that were standing in a cluster with them in front of the bar they just walked out of. It was the same bar that the hotel manager said they would be at and it was the same bar that the 50/50 crew pulled directly in front of, with malice in their hearts and blood in their eyes!

BBBRRBBRRRBBRR! BBRRRBRRBBRRAAPPPP! BBRRAPPBRAP! BRAP! BRRAAPPRATTTATTTATTTRATTABRBRBRAAPPP! BOOM! BOOM! Speechless threw two hand grenades towards the crowd of motherfuckers across the street that were a little too deep, about thirty of them little punk motherfuckers.

BBRRAAAPPPBRRRAAPPPPBBBRRRAAAPPP!   BBRRAAPP! BRRAP! RAATATATATATATATATAT! RATATATATATATATAAT! RATATAATRATATATATAT!   BRRRRRBRBRBRBRRBRBRBRRRR! BRBRBRBRBRBBRRRRR!

Mountains of empty gun shells piled up outside of cars on both sides as the 50/50 Crew squeezed shots off with absolutely no remorse for their enemies. Suddenly, the car doors opened up on both vehicles with Speechless, Pretty Boy, Gorilla, and Chinky all emerging and shooting whoever was running or standing. A few of the young soldiers attempted to shoot back at the 50/50 Crew as they saw the 50/50 Crew heading towards where their bosses had fallen, but their attempts were feeble. The firepower that the 50/50 Crew was armed with was just too much for The Terribles. They were caught completely off guard when the war was brought to <u>their</u> doorstep, and they paid dearly with their lives. The 50/50 Crew approached the heap of wounded and dead bodies as they reloaded their weapons, then they proceeded to fill the bodies with more bullet holes until no one was moving or moaning. Sirens blared in the distance. Turning around to finish the gunfight, Chinky and Pretty Boy started to shoot the goons that were trying to run up and possibly squeeze off a lucky shot or two, while Gorilla and Speechless threw concussion grenades towards the gunners coming from the other end of the street, ending their lives instantly. After the explosions, Speechless and Gorilla started to shoot shit up as well, clearing the block of any and everybody representing The Terribles crew!

Aside from the several bullet wounds that the luxury rental cars sustained, the 50/50 Crew was all intact. Both Chinky and Pretty Boy had taken bullets in the gun battle, but they were absorbed by the body armor worn by all of the bosses in the family, as well as more than a few shooters in the 50/50 Crew also. Only experiencing a mild shortness of breath after being shot, each of them just shook it off and kept banging-out with the remaining advancing enemy shooters. The police sirens grew louder.

"Let's go! Clean this shit up, time to motivate!" yelled Speechless to his partners in crime. With that said, each of the 50/50 Crew let off a furious burst of gunfire, around fifteen to twenty shots each, then they each took out two grenades and threw them through the windows and open doorways of any storefront or house in the immediate area where The Terribles dwelled and used as headquarters. As soon as the grenades began to blow, the 50/50 Crew kept on shooting it out with the remaining stragglers that hid behind cars and other structures taking shots at them, hoping they would mortally wound one of the killers that had invaded their circumference as they made it to their cars, killing several more of them. Two cop cars turned the corner at a high speed as the 50/50 Crew stood just beside their cars getting ready to get in and drive off. Immediately, Chinky and Pretty boy turned their weapons towards the cruisers and began firing! When the police cars both turned on an angle and came to a halt, Speechless signaled to Gorilla.

"Gorilla NOW!" barked Speechless. On cue and with expert precision, Gorilla took out two of his grenades one by one, and quickly threw them through the windows of each car like a professional baseball pitcher. Within seconds the cruisers exploded simultaneously.

As soon as they screeched off from the scene, two final grenades were tossed far behind each of the sports cars and underneath nearby parked cars and trucks, in the event that they were followed by anyone, they needed a clean getaway.

While the 50/50 Crew bosses were putting in work killing off the leaders of The Terribles, their soldiers were carrying out one of the most murderous and bloodiest attacks that region of Florida had ever seen. Half of them all targeted the given locations of most of the Diamond Dolls and their exposed relatives, while the other half of the murderous mob set out to eliminate other members of The Terribles and their relatives whose whereabouts were disclosed by the hotel/resort manager they had interrogated, tortured, and then killed.

The plan that the 50/50 Crew bosses came up with worked perfectly, and the shooters and killers they were bringing up under their wings were truly true to their craft. Down to give their lives for the cause, and the longevity of the 50/50 Crew dynasty if need be. They weren't suicidal at all, they were simply loyal and all of them had that "kill, or be killed" instinct.

When they pulled up to the specific areas that they were ordered to obliterate, the younger soldiers in the 50/50 Crew executed everything perfectly. They <u>knew</u> that a whole lot was riding on this mission, as far as being top-priority and all, and they individually knew that they would be held accountable for their failure as well as recognized for their triumph should the annihilation be a success.

Everything from the storefronts and businesses that served as stash-spots for The Terribles, to the personal addresses belonging to members of <u>both</u> enemy factions. The Terribles and their bitches, the

Diamond Dolls, were destroyed, along with their families and loved ones. Those victims that didn't die by the bullet, perished in the fire-bombings. A total of 214 victims in all, according to the authorities a week later in the news. After searching through the rubble and sifting through all of the mountains of ashes, not one occupant survived any of the storefront or residential attacks in the numerous Miami areas. It was as though the plan of "Operation Elimination" was carried out at the most perfect time, almost perfect anyway.

What the bosses of the 50/50 Crew or their soldiers didn't know, was that Bullet of The Terribles crew and his girlfriend Goldie of the Diamond Dolls, weren't even in the area when all of the shit went down with their families in Miami. They were miles away in Tampa, Florida for a private retreat and some well-deserved quality time together. They were both shocked and burning with anger after they heard about all of the mayhem, death, and destruction brought to their gangs and their families. Never in a thousand years could either of them imagine a retaliation of this magnitude.

As they made their way back to South Beach, they decided that they would lay-low for a while together and just stay below the radar then gradually rebuild their respective families back up somehow. They would survive, and when they were strong again, the New Jersey crew responsible for this permanent pain that they both shared, would surely pay with their lives!

The 50/50 Crew and their entire team were back in Newark, New Jersey the next night after the multiple slaughters in Miami, Florida. They were satisfied with the retaliation mission, and the results of their efforts.

All of the killings and bombings were videotaped from the addresses on the front of the places, to the devastation during the assaults, by two (2) designated videographers with the soldiers of their organization. Little Crazy Brian, who was the younger cousin of Uzi Malik and had been with the 50/50 Crew since Shotgun Shawn and Uzi Malik were first inducted into the crew and became shooters/soldiers, was appointed to videotape the slayings of the Diamond Dolls and their families while Ramon, a young Latino warrior from out of Irvington, was designated to video the deaths of the remaining members from The Terribles gang and their families!

Once they were back and comfortable in their town, and once they saw the continuous news coverage of the slaughters, they were ready to watch the videos and bear witness to the retribution and wrath of their own vengeance revenge for Melissa and Diablo.

According to the news reporters, there were over sixty people murdered that day of the raid on The Terrible main turf, where their leaders were massacred, and an additional hundred and forty murders were committed against the other crew members of The Terribles, the Diamond Dolls, and their families. Over two hundred people in all, ranging in various ages, genders, and nationalities as it was declared after the autopsies revealed this via dental records. The Chief Medical Examiner also concluded that several of the houses and businesses bombed in the attacks must have completely collapsed because they found multiple corpses cluttered in several of the basements. It was declared the most malicious act perpetrated by anyone, even those responsible for the murders during the Cocaine Wars of the nineteen-eighties.

As far as Speechless, Gorilla, Chinky, and Pretty Boy were concerned, they could care fucking less! They didn't give a fuck about anything, and as far as emotions were concerned, they were numb, and only had feelings for their dead little sister Melissa, and her husband Diablo.

Out of all the shooters and gunfire exchanged, the 50/50 Crew only suffered one casualty; Little "Rock-head" Ricky from 16th Avenue, and the team also had five wounded but not seriously. Rock-head Ricky caught a bullet to the forehead, as he peeked up from behind a parked car during a shoot-out with some of the captains out of The Terribles crew. The extremely lethal grain of bullet blew out the back of his skull, even though when it entered, the entry hole was very small.

The 50/50 Crew was able to determine that they had wiped-out The Terribles crew and their female counterparts, The Diamond Dolls as well. They checked and cross-checked the names, nicknames, and tattoos revealed by the media, with the photos and information provided by Richard, the hotel/resort manager they tortured, interrogated, and then killed. They now knew, that the following members of their enemy crews were deceased: Paco, Money Moe, Mohawk, Demon, Two-Face, Troublesome, Devil, Demon, Devious,

Menace, Nightmare, No-Good, Problem, Real Raw Deal, Skinny Slim, Sniper, Goonie, Viper, Thugger, and Renegade. All of The Terribles crew. They also knew the identities of the Diamond Dolls that were killed as well. According to the news footage and the evidence recorded the by hitters on the 50/50 Crew's team, they were as follows: Silver, Sequin, Pearl, Precious, Turquoise, Opal, Platinum, Jade, Peridot, Amethyst, and Onyx.

The only one left alive out of their crew, was Goldie, as was Bullet, the only one left from The Terribles crew. They all were declared dead, but a few were very badly mutilated as well. Once the bosses of the 50/50 Crew watched the footage themselves, they could see that the shooters specifically pulled Jade and Onyx out from the back of the nail salon they co-owned together and used as one of their main legitimate businesses, and executed immediately after stating who they were and revealing their identity at gunpoint. Once they stated who they were, they were each shot in the back of the head twice and their business was burned to the ground. Their families were all located and violently murdered, as well as the family members of The Terribles crew. Either they were shot on sight or they were burned to death by one of the many fire-bombings. Each and every member of The Terribles and the Diamond Dolls were forced to reveal themselves to the video camera in their faces before they were killed. Some of them did this proudly, while others were very reluctant to cooperate, but eventually were persuaded to give up their alias.

Speechless, Chinky, Pretty Boy, and Gorilla all sat there watching the videos of the slaughters in Miami on a large 90-inch flat-screen television, smoking on the best loud Essex County had to offer. They knew this because they were the ones that brought it in and sipping on the most expensive cognac. It was a celebration! Even though, loved ones lost their lives behind this war they were in, it still was a celebratory victory for them for avenging Melissa, Diablo, Uzi Malik, and the Twins. The Butcher Boys, The Pocahontas Mamas, The Terribles, The Diamond Dolls, and the Nigerians were no more! All dealt with, dead and gone; a motherfucking memory.

They watched the videos over and over, and over again, until it was time to get rid of all the evidence against them. Then they collectively incinerated the videotapes and the video cameras.

Chapter 16
The Time Has Come

A few weeks after the slaughter in Miami, while everyone was keeping it business as usual in the 50/50 Crew, the empire began to show tremendous growth in all areas: Marijuana, Cocaine, and Heroin. Speechless and his partners in the 50/50 Crew were talking about expansion, and some of the potential states and cities they should reach out to. Miami, Florida and Albany, New York were definitely on the top of the list amongst the few mentioned.

Speechless had to consider these moves, and he also had to deal with the loose ends involving his now deceased adopted brother, Tito Calversero, and the newly released from prison, Joseph Canelli Jr. He would have to take care of this business quickly.

On the other side of town, where the Italians dominated in population and power, Joseph Canelli Jr. relished in his new position, and continued to punish anyone not affiliated with his family or under their umbrella of protection. He really was out of control, and didn't know how to cope with the fact that the woman who had caused him to go to prison was still alive out there somewhere! He was infuriated and would not sleep, could not sleep, until she was taken care of and no longer a living and breathing person walking this earth. She was dead! He would constantly tell himself daily. He decided that he would rather get rid of her sooner than later, because it was eating at his conscious so much, being that he had promised himself one of the very first things to do whenever he did get out of prison, was to kill Officer Patricia Blackwell and he just couldn't sleep well until she was a memory.

Joey Jr. summoned his most trusted goons two days later, and he gave all four of them an order. It was the same order, "Follow that police bitch until the opportunity presented itself, then grab her up and bring her to their Don alive!" The Don, Joseph Canelli, Jr. specifically stated that <u>he</u> wanted to be the one to put the bullet in her head that ended her being on this planet and he couldn't wait until they brought her to him!

There was a lot that came with the job of running an illegal enterprise of any kind, but being the head of a family in the mob was ten times that responsibility and ten times as <u>stressful</u> if you let it. One of Joey Jr.'s main ways of coping with the stress was to visit his grandfather's gravesite at their family mausoleum in Wayne, New Jersey. He would sit there, while two bodyguards would stand in the distance but still close by, and he would chat with his grandfather, the late Don Vito Canelli. He would have one-way conversations with him, where he would just spill his guts about any and everything and he would ask his grandfather to forgive him for the way he was carrying on as head of the family. He would also tell his grandfather that he had missed him very much and wished he was still here alive with him, so that he could give him wisdom and guidance while he ran the family business. He would stay for two, maybe even three hours sometimes when he got away to his grandfathers' gravesite.

The other way Joey Canelli Jr. dealt with his stress was killing! Cold-blooded murder! He would personally deal with those that needed to be erased if they were of the status of Underboss or above. He thrived on ending their lives right after they had begged him for mercy. Of course, mercy was never granted, no matter how much money, property, or territory they had offered him in exchange for their lives! He had always been a killer, his father knew this, and so did his grandfather, the former Don of the Canelli Crime Family. In his mind, getting his hands bloodied was all a part of the business, and the more you were ready to get bloody, the more you wanted the top spot on the totem pole. Immediately upon his release, all of the bosses feared what he was capable of, because he was a <u>very</u> loose cannon.

Officer Patricia Blackwell was very optimistic and patient so when it came time for her to get promoted once again, she was not only ready for the upgrade, but she had been anticipating the opportunity to become a lieutenant for quite some time now. She had taken the exam once in the past and aced-it, but she wasn't mentally ready for the career leap and when the test came around again, she passed with flying colors and decided that she wanted to wear bars and <u>give</u> orders. Now, here she was getting ready to be promoted and receive her brass bars, as well as her new salary and all of the perks that came with the upgrade, such as: a new office, new desk, a secretary, and the position to boss around those that had belittled or picked with her indirectly when she had first joined the force years ago.

She wanted Speechless to attend her promotion ceremony, but he was very busy handling business and taking care of what needed to be taken care of around town. She understood now, and she was willing to work with him until he gave up the game for good and was done with the criminal life, because she loved him very much and couldn't see herself with anyone else in life. She was more than just in LOVE with him, she was in debt to him because he had saved her life and protected her when she didn't even know she was being covered by him. When he got back from his business trip in Florida, she was going to press him about having a <u>baby</u> and settling down as a family. She still wanted to pursue and maintain her career in law enforcement, and eventually retire young and live off of savings and investments but she wasn't too sure that Kelvin would want her to still be a cop if you was compelled to leave the game alone for good at her request.

Still, she was determined to get what she wanted.

Unbeknownst to Patricia, Speechless had been home for at least two weeks already before he had finally shown himself, because he moved a certain kind of way and he did not want any drama following him home and to his doorstep. He took the fourteen days to deal with the situation with his 50/50 Crew and the after-war rituals that they did, such as: drink, smoke, celebrate, and plan to take over the defeated enemies' territory. He wanted to make sure that no person could have possibly tailed them in <u>any</u> way from Florida, so he just crashed at his bedroom at one of their many stash houses/headquarters, and when he wanted some pussy, he just went and got a suite near the airport and called up one of his few side-pieces. He was always cautious and moved the opposite of reckless because he went from a young drug dealer, to an assassin all while he was still a teenager, so being careless and reckless was not an option for him. He was <u>always</u> serious.

There was so much to do, as they were coming down from the adrenaline rush they received whenever they annihilated a rival crew or organization, and getting back to business. The Nigerians had created a tremendous void in several areas, that hustlers now considered open markets because they had supplied so many blocks and sections with pure heroin, and now that they were gone, it was anybody's opportunity, or so they thought! The 50/50 Crew immediately put their work and team on each and every block that the Nigerians had control over, and they had intentions on branching out to the areas in Florida, and upstate New York that they knew the Nigerians had influence over.

Soon, the 50/50 Crew would have to defend their new territories against up-and-coming hustlers, rival gangs that made their income mostly from the drug trade, and bosses from neighboring states such as: New York, Pennsylvania, and Maryland trying to relocate and capitalize on the millions of dollars being made every year from the heroin trade in Newark, New Jersey. They didn't care about war, they had been killing drug dealers and taking over territories for years now as a unit, a family, as brothers. They missed their comrade in arms Shorty Slice tremendously, and they would never forget him, by keeping their empire going from now 'til now on! They would run their shit as any empire or billion-dollar conglomerate was ran, and they would elect their successors when they were very old men.

Patricia waited for her man to enter their residence with the utmost anticipation, and when he walked in, she was all over him, doing all of the things that women do to keep their man satisfied. She was very impressive and he had seen her in this state in the past before. It was rare, but when it went down she was very uninhibited with it! They showered, and then went at it again twice more, before relaxing with a bowl of assorted fruit chunks feeding them to one another. As they lay there in bed watching the movie Deep Cover (one of their favorite movies) on the gigantic 120-inch screen flat-screen embedded into their bedroom wall, Patricia couldn't help but to take advantage of this opportunity, being that the atmosphere was so tranquil and calm. She started sucking his dick again, and when she came up for air and eye-contact she just blurted out the words,

"I'm ready to have your baby and want to get started immediately Kelvin," she spoke, looking him directly in his eyes.

"What? Say that again, Patricia. What did you just say to me?" he asked her, as a grin began to form at his mouth.

"I said that I want to have your baby fathead!" replied Patricia, still looking him square in the eye as she said it.

"Did you just say that you want to have a baby with me?" Speechless asked her, still smiling as he asked the question.

"Yes, that is exactly what I asked you, and I am waiting on a response to my question!" she expressed, with a sly smirk at the corners of her lips.

"I've wanted to do that for quite some time now. It would give me another reason to settle down and fall back a little from everything besides you," he lied.

"All I have ever wanted, was to be your wife and give you children. Let's start now baby, we had plenty of money," Patricia pressed.

Speechless did NOT miss that! She wanted him out of the game. That was her hidden agenda and the reason for all of this baby talk all of a sudden. He went along of course.

"We can get stared right now if you like Patricia. You want a boy or a girl? Get that ass up in the air!" he commanded as he turned her onto her stomach and entered her again from behind.

Meanwhile, on the other side of town near Bloomfield, New Jersey, Joseph Canelli Jr. was preparing his master plan of revenge against the bitch cop that had cost him some precious time out of his life. He had assembled his hit squad and they had their instructions: "Get that bitch at any cost, and do not kill her!" is what Joey Jr. had told them. He wanted to choke the existence out of her personally, while she looked into his eyes and begged for her life.

Pretty Boy, Chinky, and Gorilla were out regulating their areas and collecting money as usual. Gorilla was covering the trap spots in Irvington, Weequahic, Hillside, and Maplewood while Chinky collected from areas like Prince Street, South Orange Avenue, near East Orange, Irvine Turner Blvd., and Vailsburg and Pretty Boy picked up money from Vaux Hall, South Orange, North Newark, and the entire Ironbound Section (South Newark). Since they had returned from their trip to Miami, things were tremendously better for the team, and the areas they had inherited when they got rid of the Nigerians were producing quadruple than they were when the Africans controlled shit! Every boss in the 50/50 Crew were looking forward to branching-out and expanding their operations to different states. They had grinded from the bottom up, and had been running the streets of

Newark for many years, but it was time to increase the bank. By far, they were all millionaires and they would be set for life even if they walked away from it all and just dropped everything but they were hustlers, certified kingpins and they would never let anyone impede their progress or prevent them from accomplishing their goals of completely taking over the entire North Jersey. Sure, they had business ties with Patterson, Passaic, Elizabeth, Plainfield, and Long Branch but it wasn't the same as having complete control over those multi-million dollar producing cities.

Gorilla and Jamaica were talking about getting married, moving to Atlanta next year, and adopting either twins or a brother and sister that were younger than four or 5, because she was damaged during the time she had been kidnapped and raped, and she couldn't conceive children on her own. It was a very painful choice to except, but once she embraced the reality of not being able to give birth on her own, she vowed to love and care for a very deserving child or some truly worthy children one day, and give them all that they deserved in this life. They wanted to move away from the up north region, and relocate somewhere more secluded and serene. Somewhere in a nice southern environment, a good distance away from the fast-paced city life. She wouldn't interfere with his devotion to his 50/50 Crew, but once they moved away, he would have to either get a better fuel-efficient car or stack up on his frequent flier miles.

He had promised her that they would eventually get away far from New Jersey, she just had to be patient with him. Every day, every month, and every single year that she stayed in the state of New Jersey, was repulsive to her and she absolutely hated living there. Had it not been for her unconditional love for Gorilla, she would have been gone either to the island of Jamaica, or somewhere in the southern region of the United States for permanent relocation. She knew that they would move away one day soon, because he had always kept his promises to her ever since he had known him.

Gorilla indeed had intentions of moving his wife and future family away to somewhere safer than the area they were presently in. He grew up in Newark, New Jersey and had hustled there, flourished there, and killed there time and time again. He wasn't bailing out at all, he would never abandon his brothers and partners in crime, he just wanted his immediate loved ones to be far away from all the drama, murders, and chaos that was surely to come as they expanded their 50/50 Crew empire even wider. He may be a hustler, a boss, and an exterminator but one thing Gorilla was not, and that was stupid! He knew that there would be much more bloodshed and body-bags coming soon because they were in the killing business. It came with the territory. In order for a crew or a family in the street-life to truly excel and become a multi-million dollar entity, motherfuckers are going to be murdered. It was just a <u>fact</u> in this way of life.

Speechless knew that they were getting ready for the next level of their monopoly, which was for the 50/50 Crew to branch-out into other states and become a coastal conglomerate. He had associates in the Upstate New York areas, and also Connecticut, Florida, and Maryland already in place and on stand-by, so the 50/50 Crew would soon flood those respected areas with the best product imaginable, and wait for the inevitable results total takeover.

It wasn't that Newark was done, far from it, on the contrary it was much more money was flowing through Newark, N.J. than there had ever been in the past, but he and his crew of hustlers wanted much more for their future. The average hustlers would have been content with the success level that the 50/50 Crew had reached but this bunch was no group of ordinary paper chasers, they were the real deal, and they took no prisoners!

As soon as he handled his business with Joey Canelli Jr. and made sure that he was dead, he would give the go-ahead to his 50/50 Crew, and then reach out to his people out of state in order to implement what he called "Operation Boa Constructor," because his plan would completely smother the competition until they were dead!

In order to track down and kill Joey Canelli Jr., Speechless would have to go above and beyond his regular approach to situations. He would have to be smarter than ever, and very, very careful. He also, would need one other person to assist him on this mission, Pretty Boy.

Speechless lit up a blunt of sour, and then placed a call to Pretty Boy. He answered on the second ring.

"What's good my brother? Everything good with you?" inquired Pretty Boy.

"No my brother. Everything is not good at all, I need to see you as soon as possible Pretty Boy, it's very important bro," replied Speechless.

"Say no more, I'm there!" said Pretty Boy, before he hung up the phone in a hurry.

Pretty Boy pulled up thirty-five minutes later to one of Speechless' houses out in Short Hills.

"What the fuck is up Speechless? You got me thinking all kinds of negative shit right now!" said Pretty Boy.

"Sit down my brother. There's something you must know about your big brother Speechless," he said calmly.

Chapter 17
I Got Your Back

After Speechless revealed his secret to Pretty Boy about being a contract killer for the Italian Mob, and claiming to have had that title, that profession since they all were in their late teens. Pretty Boy was completely stunned. He could not believe what he was hearing coming out of his best friends own mouth. "Speechless? Was a contract hit-man for the motherfucking Italian mafia? No fucking way!" Pretty Boy said to himself. *No fucking way!*

"Pretty Boy, are you alright bro, you good?" Speechless asked. "I really need you to be on board with me, because THIS is what I do and have been doing for a long time. Tony Calversero was my half-brother. His father saved me, raised me, and taught me how to be a better professional and a better boss. He is the reason I am the person I am today! By mere obligation I am compelled to retaliate for the actions taken by the mafia that caused Tito and his men their lives and trust me brother, that shit WILL NOT go unanswered! I am going to need your help with this mission that I have to carry out on these very dangerous enemies of mine. There are a lot of people that are going to die behind the death of Tito, and I don't believe that I would make it out of there alive if I did this shit by myself, and believe me my brother, I have done more than many missions on my own. This is different though. This is probably more dangerous than any job I have ever been paid to do, or any war that we have been through as the 50/50 Crew when we were annihilating our foes," concluded Speechless. He looked at Pretty Boy sternly and scanned his facial reactions for some type of disapproval or disbelief but he saw none. He and Pretty Boy were like brothers, just as everyone in the 50/50 Crew were but Gorilla and Chinky both had been injured in recent wars and were still healing, despite what they might say to their fellow comrades in reference to their abilities to perform in battle. Still, this was different though, very different. Pretty Boy responded finally, after what seemed to Speechless a damn eternity

"What do we have to do brother? Who we got to kill? I'm with you Speechless, you should already know that shit," said Pretty Boy with a straight face, as he lit up a blunt.

For the next four weeks, despite it being, business as usual with the 50/50 Crew, Speechless taught Pretty Boy about being a hit-man and about the many more ways to kill someone, other than just stabbing or shooting them.

By the third week of his crash-training course, Speechless felt as though Pretty Boy had absorbed enough skills and methods. He was already sharp as a tack and had the heart of five lions, so Speechless knew that he could count on him for back-up shit he knew that before he even told Pretty Boy about his secret life. Now, it was time for the second phase of Pretty Boy's training and this on the job training part could be extremely dangerous and deadly. He would spend the next four weeks going underground, and prepping for his vital role in this murder plot.

Speechless knew that he had to eliminate Joey Jr. and destroy anyone connected to his enterprise and he knew that it would be closure for him, in more ways than one.

For the next few weeks that passed, Chinky and Gorilla made their regular rounds, doing the usual pick-ups and drop-offs, while Speechless prepared for the important task ahead of him. He had to make sure that all basis were covered and that there were no mistakes, because one small mistake could cost him, Pretty Boy, or both of them their lives. He had always been a very meticulous planner and had taken things seriously since he was a kid hustler. The results he was always successful.

He still hadn't looked into the contents of Salvatore's journal, although he anticipated what gory truths were scribed unto those pages. Still, he would be ready to investigate the private entries of his mentor as soon as his enemies were dead and gone! He had no time for distractions now.

It was time to take care of business with his connections out of town as well, but he had to first make sure that the next shipment of 8,000 kilos four thousand bricks of Columbian Fish-Scale, and four thousand bricks of China White heroin had arrived safely, and was secured in all of their stash house locations.

Three days later, the 50/50 Crew's connect made the drop successfully and they secured the product. They were ready for the next phase in their plan.

When Tito and his team were brought into the picture, by way of coming to Chinky's aid, it was the furthest thing from Speechless mind was that they would travel to New Jersey and get themselves killed. Speechless had no clue that Tito would go after Joey Canelli Jr., but Tito was a gangster, and his father had been murdered viciously at the hands of those who were employed by the Canelli Crime Family. His attempt would not go in vain, and the death of Salvatore Calzonetti would surely be avenged!

It had been three months since the deaths of Tito and his crew, it was time.

Speechless got his bag together, showered, and changed into his murder clothes, and then he lit up a blunt of sour diesel and called Pretty Boy.

"Yeah, what's up bro? You ready to roll?" asked Pretty Boy.

"Let's go brother, everything set?" asked Speechless, referring to Pretty Boy's preparation for the mission.

"Absolutely, I'm ready!" confirmed Pretty Boy, as he loaded up the last of four pistols (2 revolvers and four automatics), wrapped them individually in hand towels, and zipped them up in his backpack. He too lit up a blunt of sour, then sat back on his plush sofa smoking on the exotic weed until Speechless got there.

Gorilla and Jamaica were still planning on relocating to the state of Georgia (The "Buck Head" area to be specific), and now that things were getting ready to get heavy with the 50/50 Crew's new expansion into other states, Gorilla was even more anxious to get at least his wife Jamaica safely out of the state just in case the new enemies they acquired along the way would reach out to the family members and loved ones of their competitors. It was getting ready to be a very tough time.

Chinky was still with the same shorty he had been with ever since he had been back from Miami, when Tito Calversero, along with his team rescued him, and nurtured him back to health until his 50/50 Crew arrived to retrieve him. She laid there next to him, watching an excellent classic Irish mob movie called Miller's Crossing as he sat there on his bed counting money from the large picnic cooler he kept right next to his bed. He would always start counting the money whenever his personal stash coolers began to get full. The 50/50 Crew had a collective kiddie of over a billion dollars (cash, assets, and legit businesses), but each boss had his own bank accounts filled with profits from the game, and kept them disguised as legitimate business transactions through their various companies, because they were all listed as either "sole proprietor" of the business, or "C.E.O"., or simply a twenty percent partner Shorty Slice's wife and family still collected his 20% share of the 50/50 Crews' acquired wealth. They were good for life and then some, they were family and besides, Shorty Slice gave his life defending the 50/50 Crew's honor, and territory.

Every time that one of Chinky's coolers filled up, he would count all of the cash then wrap it up in $50,000.00 stacks, and put all the money back into the cooler, eight rows across and five stacks high. Once he had the stash cooler full, he would then plastic wrap the entire cooler at least four to five times. After that he would duct tape all four sides and the top of the cooler three to four times. When he was done, it always looked like an over-sized Christmas gift without the bow on top, the way it was wrapped up. When that was all done, the next morning or early afternoon, routinely he would take a couple of hours out of his schedule, and he would drive out to one of his properties in West Caldwell, a huge private home he owned set back into the woods just a little off the main road, with the neighbors being at least a quarter miles distance away in every direction.

At this particular property that Chinky owned, aside from the foundation to the house, there was no concrete that had been laid or poured at. Also, there was dirt everywhere, including the large three-car garage where he always kept three small vehicles inside covered up. Once he pulled up to the house, he would open up the garage door then take the tarp off of whichever car he would move, then after he backed the car up to the entrance of the garage, he would get out and get the cooler from backseat of the car he drove up there and bring it to the back wall of the garage. Once he put the cooler down, he would grab one of three shovels he kept inside of the garage and start digging a fresh hole for the money and he would always dig a hole big enough to put two coolers into the ground side by side. Over a period of about five years, he had dug and filled nine holes. This would be his tenth money pit in the morning he thought to himself, as Sheila her way over to him and began sucking on his dick while he continued to count money. Not many drug dealers alive or dead can say that they actually put up $40,000,000.00 but that was Chinky's goal, to stash that amount before the Feds or death caught up to them.

Feds, haters, local/state police, and enemies put together, could not stop the momentum of the 50/50 Crew. They had progressed fifty times over since they had started getting money together as teenagers, and the violent tsunami they rode was an unstoppable one. They were getting ready to expand their brand and soon, the 50/50 Crew would have control of 20-25% of the East Coast drug trade, controlling the majority of cocaine, heroin, and marijuana that entered Boston, Mass., Springfield, Mass., Albany, N.Y., Syracuse, N.Y., the entire Northern New Jersey, Baltimore, Maryland, Forest Park, Georgia, and Miami, Florida. All of the bosses in those areas would be killed off and replaced with 50/50 Crew captains and controlled by soldiers and shooters of the 50/50 Crew. They were all just waiting for the button to be pushed by Speechless, and the <u>slaughter</u> would commence statewide right before the flood of new drugs hit each state. First, Speechless had to take care of business and avenge Tito's death, as well as bring closure to the organization that had his teacher killed.

When Speechless arrived at the spot to pick up Pretty Boy, he could see that Pretty Boy was ready as he always was when it came time to get busy and put in work for the crew! He was beyond ready. He was focused!

"Let's go handle these motherfuckers Speechless, and hit them like they never saw us coming at their motherfucking asses!" Pretty Boy stated as he closed the door of the vehicle, right after he had placed his bag in the trunk, next to a huge arsenal of shit that Speechless had inside of there already.

"That's why it had to be you that I revealed my secret to. I already know everyone's loyalty is unquestionable in the 50/50 Crew, but you best fit the necessary part in this particular war we are about to end my brother. They will never see you coming Pretty Boy," Speechless replied as he put the gearshift in drive and pulled off casually.

The rest of the 50/50 Crew and the bosses, Gorilla and Chinky that were left behind in Newark to maintain and run things, were completely oblivious to the mission Speechless and Pretty Boy were on. They were all under the impression that Pretty Boy and Speechless went out of state to secure shit up in New York and Mass. Although they did make jokes about Pretty Boys' new look.

They didn't know that two of their dear beloved brothers were about to take on the entire faction of the Canelli Crime Family. Plus, anyone willing to take up arms and die right along with them.

Chapter 18
The Time Has Come...

They had studied the ins-and-outs and the day-to-day movements of every single member of Joey Canelli Jr.'s crew, including Joey Canelli Jr. himself, and for the last two months, even though they had plenty of opportunities to kill Joey Canelli Jr., Speechless and Pretty Boy waited because it was still part of Pretty Boy's training as a hired killer and assassin, to exercise the most extreme patience. So, instead of prematurely executing their plan just because an opportunity presented itself, they waited, and Speechless used it as one more lesson in Pretty Boy's schooling. Now, the time was upon them, and it was time to get busy killing their enemies.

Speechless and Pretty Boy had known from their weeks of stake-outs that the Canelli Crime Family had their very own casino and underground gambling operations going on, and they knew which days the casino action would be going down because Joey Canelli Jr. had gambled there almost every day of the week. Whether it was at night, in the middle of the night, or early in the a.m., he was there gambling at some point in a twenty-four-hour time period, it was almost routine. Of course, they also collected tremendous amounts of money through the casino business that they ran as a front, while they made hundreds of thousands of dollars on average every week from illegal gambling.

The plan was already discussed and rehearsed over and over again between Speechless and Pretty Boy, and they were going through with it tonight no matter what! Pretty Boy had been playing poker and shooting dice for about a month straight inside of their establishment (also part of his covert-training), and pretending to be one of the new mafia members in the area from one of the Las Vegas mafia families, and he was spending cash as if he had hit the lottery yesterday. It didn't matter whether or not he won big or lost big, as long as he attracted the attention of the gangsters that were gambling and trying to be recognized. He had shaved off all off his facial hair, and he now wore his hair slicked back and moussed into a ponytail-style, and wore nothing but the most expensive attire from the finest clothiers Downtown Newark, only the imported stuff from Italy from the suit to the shoes. He was coming in the gambling spot tonight though with murderous intentions and Pretty boy always took care of business when it came down to it. He had five thousand, one-hundred-dollar bills on him, stashed inside of his pockets and the money vest he had on over his bullet-proof and he also was armed for a war, as he carried altogether two .38 caliber automatics on each ankle, two .38 Specials that swung from shoulder holsters, and two .45 automatics tucked down in his back and strapped securely within two custom-made holsters and a back brace. Should the plan go smoothly, the two .45 automatics would be the very last guns that he used.

Speechless had the big guns out tonight, and he meant business! The business of extermination! He wasn't going to rest until he knew that he was responsible for the deaths of Joseph Canelli Jr. and anyone involved with him. Tonight, none of those motherfuckers stood a chance against the arsenal that he brought along, because according to Pretty Boy, they only kept two to three shotguns on the premises, and a couple of handguns.

His personal arsenal consisted of two hand grenades, Two MG4's equip with mounts and burlap bags to catch all of the dispensed shell casings, and a WA2000 that came with a high-powered digital 3-D scope and was loaded with armor-piercing bullets as well. The only other guns he had with him were two big ass seven-shot 357 Magnum revolvers that would clearly be useful in the event that he had to assist Pretty Boy inside of the underground casino.

Pretty Boy was known for spending and displaying large amounts of cash during the poker and dice games, and he even side-betted on whatever action was available. Again, he didn't care about winning or losing, he was just there to be noticed. On the night of the hit on the Canelli Crime family's club and casino, he and Speechless were not expecting Pretty Boy to get searched at all, because they never <u>ever</u> searched him after that initial week of him going to the spot. The more he went there, the more cash he brought with him and they always knew that he would bring a lot of money with him, even though he always had at least one burner on him after that first week of pat frisking. They didn't TRUST Pretty Boy but they were careless, and their greed for easy money would eventually be their fatal downfall.

When Speechless pulled the vehicle one block away from the scene, and directly across the street from the Canelli Crime Family's underground gambling joint, he and Pretty Boy exited, then expertly began to strap-up, swiftly arming themselves with all that they could carry, as they had rehearsed many, many times before during Pretty Boys training as an assassin.

He was known around the joint as Vincent, Vincent Palleti from Las Vegas, and that was all they needed to know about him for him to be accepted amongst the Italian gangsters and gamblers that frequented the place. He always came by himself, and left without any bodyguards or protection that they could see no matter how much money he might have walked away with on any particular night. He was respected among the Italian gangsters tremendously, because he always tipped the dealers handsomely and he never, ever complained whenever he lost. Again, that was all just a part of his cover.

Speechless and Pretty Boy headed towards the targets, and they made sure that no one saw them when they made their way through the backyards leading to the casino/club. As soon as they were directly across the street, Speechless took up position in this little doggie-park where many people walked their dogs and let them relieve themselves, but fortunately for them the timing was right, and the park was empty. Speechless quickly set up his tripod and put his equipment together as Pretty Boy made his way towards the club entrance and walked past the two, armed goons at the door, Joe and Tommy They didn't harass Pretty Boy about the fact that he looked a little heavier tonight, because it was the Fall season and cold out, so they didn't really pay any extra attention to Vincent's bulging black parka.

As soon as he was inside the casino/club, Speechless knew that Pretty Boy would waste no time at all handling his business, because they already knew that Junior was inside. He quickly assassinated the two guards dropping them with head shots. They never knew what hit them. Then, he waited for Pretty Boy's signal.

Once he was inside, Pretty Boy immediately made his way past all of the people who were greeting him and making comments trying to get his attention and see where he would be gambling at that night. Dice, Roulette, Poker, or Blackjack. He just kept it moving and kept his focus sharp. Once he entered the "V.I.P." area of the casino, where Joseph Canelli Jr. would surely be, he spotted him, then walked to the bathroom speaking to everyone on his way there. Once inside of the bathroom, he didn't waste any time. He removed of the left 38 Special from its holster, and put it in his right parka pocket and then he took out one of the grenades and removed the pin, holding down the mechanism that would allow it to go off. He then held that in his left hand inside his other parka pocket. Swiftly he left the lavish bathroom, and headed straight towards where Junior sat playing poker, with his bodyguard standing to his left. Pretty Boy didn't hesitate. He walked up to Junior as he spoke to his bodyguard, "How's it going tonight?" stated Pretty Boy, as he pulled his hands from his jacket pockets simultaneously and tossed the grenade into the lap of Joseph Canelli Jr. not waiting for an answer and shooting the bodyguard in the forehead once.

Before the grenade could explode, Pretty Boy shot Junior quickly in the face as surprise registered on his screwed mug and the grenade went off blowing him up, the impact knocking Pretty Boy temporarily off of his feet as well. The entire scene was in chaos, as patrons scattered and guns were drawn then fired in the direction of Pretty Boy. Now standing with two guns blazing, Pretty Boy found the farthest corner from the gathering and squeezed off shot after shot, emptying his revolvers, all the while making sure that he stood clear of the entrance to the V.I.P. room. He was empty and took a shot to the chest as it knocked him backwards and into the wall he was standing near. Gathering himself quickly, he caught his breath and reached for the other grenade, pulled the pin and tossed it where most of the gunfire was coming from. Before the second grenade could explode, Pretty Boy was already reaching for the two 45's that were tucked down in his back, and he started blasting away at those that were not injured or killed by the grenade blast.

The first grenade blast that went off was the signal Speechless had been waiting for and then he knew exactly what to do. As Italian mobsters came scrambling from the entrance of the club running for dear life, Speechless mercilessly unleashed a barrage of automatic gunfire that left no one alive. Round after round he held the triggers to the MG4's and just maneuvered them from side-to-side as he swept the sidewalk and the side alley adjacent to the club/casino, hitting everything he pointed towards.

Inside of the place, Pretty Boy was still fighting for survival and making his way towards the back door, because he knew by now that Speechless was outside tearing shit up with those big guns that he brought along, and soon he would be entering the club to destroy it, had he not heard from Pretty Boy.

The V.I.P. Room was completely destroyed, and everywhere the eye could see there was gun smoke and broken glass. Small fires had been started also from the grenade blasts and Pretty Boy knew that it was most definitely time to get up outta there quick, fast, and in a hurry! He reloaded his 45 automatics, barely getting a chance to take a breath before some goon or another came running from one of the corners or hidden places shooting. Pretty Boy didn't stop punishing anyone standing, because his intentions was to kill Junior Canelli and anyone in the immediate area with him, that meant everyone in the entire fucking clubhouse/casino. As he shot his way through to the back of the spot, working his way to the rear exit, he ran out of ammo in the 45 automatics. Then from nowhere, someone rushed him with a football tackle and damn near knocked the wind out of him, blindsiding him with pain. When he regained his wits about him, Pretty Boy realized that it was one of the bigger goons that hung around the club for muscle, trying to get stripes for putting in work. Pretty Boy landed two quick left uppercuts to the thugs chin, then a right elbow to his jaw knocking him to the ground. Before he could grab his icepick, he remembered the baby twin 380 caliber automatics he wore on each ankle. Grabbing the right one, he squeezed off three rapid rounds into the big goons head and neck, then he grabbed the other one from its holster and kept shooting until he heard heavy automatic gunfire coming from the other gambling room towards the front of the casino. It was Speechless! It had to be because Pretty boy was almost out of bullets.

"Pretty boy! Where are you, Bro? Pretty Boy give me a holler or something, Bro! He could hear Speechless yelling for him in between the rapid concessions of heavy gunfire.

"I'm back here, brother. Just follow my voice!" Pretty Boy yelled back at him, as he shot the last of his 380 clip, hearing and feeling the chamber click empty. Then, as he reached and removed his icepick to prepare for hand-to-hand combat, he was suddenly hit in in back by a shotgun blast! The impact had sent him flipping forwards and completely off of his feet, because he was trying to stand up when he was hit.

"AAHHHHHH Shit! I'm hit!" he screamed out in agony as the blast punched him hard, bruising his spine and right kidney but not penetrating his vest at all. "I'm fucking hit Speech!" He screamed out again in pain after he landed and caught his breath louder this time so that Speechless could hear him and follow the direction of his voice. Then, the loud submachine gunfire grew louder, and closer, and Pretty Boy could see bodies dropping as he scrambled to get to his feet, the icepick still clutched in his right hand but he was hurt real bad. He stabbed at the closest body to him, whether they were armed with a gun, weapon, or not. He just poked away as people ran towards him or tried to run past him frantically.

"I see you, Bro! Get down!" Speechless yelled as he sprayed the rest of the room that Pretty Boy was trapped in, hitting every target and cutting people to shreds as Pretty Boy dropped flat to the floor. "Where's the back door, Pretty Boy?" Speechless yelled to him, quickly turning around to gun down two goons running up shooting revolvers at him. The bullets hit him twice, one striking him in the center of his chest, and the other one hitting him in the left upper thigh area before he cut the guys down. He was protected with body armor from neck to shins, so none of the slugs penetrated his flesh. "Motherfuckers!" Speechless yelled out as the slugs hit him and he returned fire. "Back door?" He asked Pretty Boy again.

Once Pretty Boy pointed towards the backdoor, Speechless took out one of his own grenades, pulled the pin and tossed it towards the base of the backdoor. It blew open with shards of the door and wall flying everywhere it sight. Then Pretty Boy scrambled to his feet, and joined his brother Speechless in the battle. Speechless handed Pretty Boy one of the seven-shot 357's that he had on him because Pretty Boy was in no position to shoot both guns, he was bruised up badly. Pretty Boy then put away his ice pick and proceeded to grip the huge revolver with both hands, and then they shot their way out of the back door and kept on shooting until they were standing in the backyard area of the club, where most of the Italians would smoke and mingle, or grill food on nice weather days. No one was back there on this particular night though. Everyone had cleared the area after hearing all of the gunfire and explosions, and the few that had planned on trying to ambush Pretty Boy and Speechless on their way out of the back entrance, were blown up when Speechless threw the grenade at the bottom of the backdoor.

"Pretty Boy come on let's go! Can you run bro?" Speechless asked him, as he broke into a stride and started away from the club/casino, still gripping his WA2000, and pointing it at anyone but Pretty Boy as they made their escape towards the ride they came in. They could hear shots in the distance behind them, and hear a few bullets wiz pass them, but not one hit them.

Once they were close to the car, Speechless automatically opened the truck by remote control and they tossed the weaponry into the trunk then drove off as if a massacre didn't just take place a block away.

Once the smoke had cleared, and all of the dust was settled, there were 41 people that lost their lives that night inside the walls of the casino/club that was owned by the Canelli Crime Family, including Joseph Canelli Jr, who's body was barely recognizable amidst the wreckage. D.N.A. tests and dental records confirmed that it was indeed him, and news reports confirmed at least twenty-five of the deceased to be members of the Canelli Crime Family's organization as well.

Although, Speechless was more than confident in Pretty Boy's ability to carry out the task of eliminating Joey Canelli Jr., the news report was the specific proof that Speechless was waiting to hear for official confirmation. Now, his mentor and his brother Tito Calversero could rest in peace. He was ready to move on with the 50/50 Crews' plan to take over multiple states and expand!

Gorilla was very successful in moving his wife Jamaica out of the state of New Jersey and to Atlanta without any mishaps or incidents with any enemies. They settled on a huge home that had measured at

57,000 square feet and had two swimming pools, an indoor as well as an outdoor pool. Also, the driveway was at least a quarter mile drive from the main street to their mini-mansion. It boasted a four-car garage and cathedral ceilings throughout the home that proudly displayed beautiful crystal chandeliers, as well as two spiral staircases leading to the upstairs. It was absolutely beautifully painted already when Jamaica fell in love with it, and once Gorilla ordered all of the furniture it was even more beautiful now that it was complete. She KNEW that he could not stay home for too long, and that he and his 50/50 Crew had unfinished business up in New Jersey and New York. She knew that he would leave soon, and be right back in the same dangerous environment they strived to get away from by geographically relocating and getting a fresh start. She knew her man, and she knew that he was loyal to his friends.

Pretty Boy and Chinky decided to relocate their families down south to Naples, Florida where it was serene and lavish, but at the same time it was also quite and subtle. They brought huge homes that were next door to one another and kept their families close because they were already like brothers way before the 50/50 Crew even formed, so they would keep it that way forever. Across the street from them, was the widow and children of their fallen comrade, Shorty Slice, and next to her home was a large house for Pretty Boys' niece and nephew, his murdered sisters' kids, to grow up in when they got older.

Speechless decided on Marietta, GA for his new residency. It was of course plush and lavish, and a gift to himself and Patricia but he still kept one of his favorite homes in New Jersey, out in Short Hills as did Chinky with his stash house out in the woods. His lavish, extravagant home was just as big as Gorillas' house was, and his showed off "his and hers" Range Rovers, plus "his and hers" CL 600 Mercedes Benz coupes, in the enormous driveway. His deck in the rear of the home was big enough to comfortably park at least three cars on it, and its' rooms were all presidential in size, cathedral ceilings and all.

They set up businesses in both Florida and the state of Georgia, just as they had done back home in Newark, New Jersey.

Everything with their connections out of town was all good, and the 50/50 Crew was ready to reach out to Upstate New York, Mass.,

Connecticut, Maryland, and Florida and capitalize on the tremendous market that was getting ready to open up. Their murder squads were set and in place. Soon, many streets in five different states would be covered in blood and empty bullet shells, all because of the 50/50 Crew.

Epilogue

The only remaining Nigerian gangster left alive had no doubt survived an onslaught that he was very lucky to have avoided because it had killed his entire crew and any witnesses to the crime except for two people. He knew that it was imperative that he made it back to the Motherland, so that he could regroup and heal his severe injuries. He vowed to return and avenge his brothers and the rest of the people that meant anything to him who died in the wars against the 50/50 Crew. He was there, inside of the vault when the two white girls came running and screaming and cowered for shelter within the confines of the reinforced space. He saw them, looked right at them but they couldn't see him, for he was hiding himself, covered up by an old painters' tarp. He stood by whilst his comrades and brothers were annihilated and killed off by the 50/50 Crew.

Leopard saw them all. He knew who was responsible for his brothers deaths and he would bide his time until it was safe, then he would strike again, for his brothers and his pride! He waited for the two Canadian white girls to leave, watched them leave, let them leave, then after an hour had passed by, he himself left the smoldering remains of the Nigerians secret lair limping away, but he was still alive.

When the two remaining females of the Chinchillas Crew made it safely back to Canada, they immediately shared the story about the wars, the deaths and their survival run to get back home. All of the remaining Chinchillas were eager to get revenge for their fallen sisters. They were just as dedicated as any gang member, Anywhere U.S.A., and they would surely see the streets of Newark, New Jersey, and the 50/ fifty Crew again, guaranteed.

THE END

Turn the page for a sneak preview of the follow-up to this epic sequel.

Switch Hitter Part 3: Salvatore's Journal

Prologue

Speechless sat in the confines of his huge basement…his "man-cave" underneath his new plush Georgia home, and lightly brushed off the cloth wrapping that held the diary of his slain teacher and mentor the legendary mafia hit man: Salvatore Calzonetti, and then he began to open the journal reading its' first page, realizing that it was addressed to him. It read:

My beloved apprentice and son Speechless, since the beginning of our introduction in was destiny for you to be my student, and for me to return the favor of you assisting me when I was in distress, even though I could've killed those four youths easily. I took great pleasure and pride in teaching you and altering your life by giving you a different perspective on how to approach life's situations. The gift I gave you, was one that I didn't even bestow upon my own biological son Tito, and he was a young gangster far before I was aware of it. Still, he was not chosen to be my extended arm to the murder-for-hire game; you were that hand-picked person. We have made a lot of money together throughout the years we have known one another, and we have completed many journeys as well throughout your training, graduation, and grad school. Now the time is upon us, and if you are reading this journal then I am indeed dead and gone, and more than likely it was a very violent death, because I will never go quietly and without a good fight.

Speechless began to shed tears of anger, as he reminisced about his mentor and what a great man he was.

"I want you to do three things for me my son: The first, is to avenge my death, and see to it that those responsible are dealt with accordingly. The second thing, is to find out what happened to my beautiful Sylvia and if she is alive, please find my beloved daughter. And the third and final thing I ask of you my son, is to carry out all of this unfinished business detailed in this

journal.

There are people, families, and even organizations that should no longer be, but they are still here because I did not or could not finish the job for some reason. Below, there is a detailed list of all of the targets that need to be eliminated so that I can rest in peace. I know...it is a very extensive list Speechless, but this is what you were trained to do, and this completes your debt to me. Thank You, my Son.

Speechless just sat there, looking at the page in the journal with all of those names and locations on and he couldn't believe that Salvatore had spared so many, and had left all these jobs incomplete. He lit up a blunt of sour diesel, sat back, and thought deeply about the many tasks at hand.

Meanwhile, on another side of Lake Ontario, The Chinchillas were in full force and had reached record numbers, totaling ninety-two females in all, and every last one of them were willing to die for the cause of being respected and recognized as a Chinchilla. They were still infuriated behind the news of their deceased sisters-in-arms, and they all sharpened and updated whatever deadly skills they possessed while waiting for the chance to strike back and kill all of those responsible.

They grew in business and sold three times as much weed as they normally did, because they were in a rush to purchase new weapons plus the information, they would need in order to track down their enemies was not going to be cheap at all. So, they needed money to throw around and get answers to certain questions they would surely be asking in the near future. They had secured a new gun connect back in the states, near the DMV area and the people they were going to be dealing with came highly recommended by some really street certified people in Canada.

They had all decided that only twelve of them would stay back home in Canada, just in case but the remaining eighty would travel ten at a time over to Newark, New Jersey. They would make eight different trips, but they would all make it there safely, and set up shop until the time came for retributionand this time, they would be ready!

Leopard had safely escaped New Jersey as well and had made it back to Nigeria and was healing and regaining his strength for a while, but now, he was on his way back to the United States of America with his new crew, The Body Snatchers, who were all the little wild ass cousins, brothers, and jailhouse friends of the slain members in the Nigerian Crew. They were a ruthless bunch that didn't care about anything, or anyone.

Now they were headed to the United States with their leader, the last remaining member of the original Nigerian Dope Boys Crew that ruled half of Newark's dope trade for decades under most noses. They were ready for their slice of the American Dream the same dream that became a reality for their older deceased relatives and friends.

Chapter 1
Fulfilling A Promise

Speechless sat patiently, waiting for his third victim in a month to come out of their place of comfort, and as soon as that happened, he would cut their life short with a bullet. He had to get back into the flow of things for the promise he had made, to honor Salvatore's dying wish and complete all of the contracts that Salvatore left undone.

He got right to it, and began handling his business with tracking them down and doing all the recon himself. He didn't request help from Pretty Boy on these. He had these contracts. Then, he one by one killed them off with an assassins' bullet to the back or the front of the head. He had chosen to use his snipers' rifle for the first twenty kills of the 75 unfulfilled contracts left behind by Salvatore, and he would terminate them as a special tribute to his mentor for the snipers rifle, was Salvatore's favorite weapon of choice to exterminate with.

After today, he would have seventeen more kills to go, and then he could switch it up from the snipers' rifle to something else.

He lay on top of the loose gravel on the roof that was directly across the street from where his target had once lived freely, but had now only frequented every so often, sneaking in and out of the plush playpen. Speechless knew all of this from tailing him for days that turned into two weeks. As soon as Filipe Nabarros, who was an informant for the Feds emerged from his condo, Speechless blew his brains all over the wall of his building next to the doors entrance.

After the third completed contract, Speechless left Colorado and headed back to Georgia via private jet, and as usual, his flight was smooth and trouble-free.

He got home safely after being gone for over a month, and was greeted by Patricia at the door. She had a look of grief on her face. As soon as he kissed then embraced her, the floodgate of tears began to pour from her eyes and soak his torso as she squeezed him.

"Baby, what is it? What's the matter with you sweetheart? What the hell has you crying like this?" Speechless demanded, as he looked down at her. She then pulled away from him a little, still in his arms, then glared up at him with her pretty face smeared with tears and with her voice shaking. She told him the gruesome news about her entire families' murder, and the people claiming responsibility for the violation.

"They call themselves the Body Snatchers!" she yelled out as she screamed and cried at the same time, her voice trembling, thinking about her Mother, Father, Grandmother, and two teenage brothers, that were all destroyed by these monsters!

Speechless grabbed her close, kissed her on the forehead and quietly promised her revenge as he stared at himself in the mirror.

ABOUT THE AUTHOR

Karriem Bilal Muhammad, is a Newark, New Jersey native whose Muslim background has kept him well-balanced and focused. He aspires to change the lives of those around him by being successful and encouraging others to reach their dreams.

He founded his own publishing company, Move The Chains Publishing, with a focus on urban fiction literature. His first novel *Switch Hitter*, the first in his series of four total works.

Karriem is on the road to being a notable name in Urban Fiction and Black Authored literature.

Made in the USA
Middletown, DE
23 October 2024